Jefferson's Saddle

It is meant to be a day of celebration in Mortimer, Texas, but everything changes when Charlie Jefferson arrives in town. Left for dead after a brutal ambush and robbery, Charlie is intent on finding the man who did this to him.

En route to Mortimer from the wastelands where he was left to perish, Charlie stumbles upon a dying Texas Ranger. Unwittingly, he is drawn into a plot involving the town's council.

By showing mercy, Charlie becomes part of the plot, whether it ties in with his plans or not. Charlie's mission in Mortimer is no longer personal. The fate of the whole town rests with him.

Jefferson's Saddle

Will DuRey

A Black Horse Western

ROBERT HALE · LONDON

ISBN 978-0-7198-1682-6

Robert Hale Limited
Clerkenwell House
Clerkenwell Green
London EC1R 0HT

www.halebooks.com

Typeset by
Derek Doyle & Associates, Shaw Heath
Printed and bound in Great Britain by
CPI Antony Rowe, Chippenham and Eastbourne

CHAPTER ONE

Pistol in hand, the man stepped out from behind the bush. He was dust-covered, like a man who had spent several hours on the trail, and the redness of his face confirmed that he had been a long time in the sun. He was a thickset man in well-worn range clothes. The fabric of his stained grey Stetson had been softened by exposure to too many storms and its brim now drooped where it should have formed channels to drain away rainwater. The pocket of his blue shirt was ripped and his black trousers were tucked into scuffed brown boots. He had thick eyebrows over small, dark eyes, and when he spoke his thick lips seemed to curl in a habitual sneer, forming his features into a testament of cruelty.

'If you make me shoot again I'll blast you clean out of the saddle.'

The voice was rough and the words heavy with threat, but heeding them wasn't Charlie Jefferson first priority. The unexpected first shot had seared his upper left arm which, in addition to inducing a yell of pain, threw a spurt of dark blood into the air and, under him, the combined noises of his shout and the nearby gunshot caused the young horse to skitter, so that it twisted and hopped as it struggled to escape the restraint that Charlie was trying to impose. A shortened rein caused the red gelding to rear high, almost unseating Charlie, but when once more it had all four feet on the ground it accepted his control although not without a series of snuffles and nervous shivers.

The ambusher spoke again. 'Get down,' he ordered, jiggling his gun to emphasize the command. 'I'm taking your horse.'

Although reluctant to dismount, Charlie paused for only a second. The perils for a stranger cast afoot in this barren territory were obvious but the alternative was sure death. The hammer on the gunman's pistol was pulled fully back and the scowl on his face made it clear that he wouldn't hesitate to pull the trigger to get what he wanted. But, Charlie figured, if killing him had been the gunman's main intention then he would already have done so, so he swung his leg over the horse's back and stepped down, wincing slightly as he gripped the saddle horn.

The man stepped forward, grabbed the gelding's lead rein with his left hand, looped it around his wrist, then pulled the horse towards him. At the same time he motioned with his pistol for Charlie to move further away. When they were about twenty feet apart, he issued another command.

'Carefully,' he told Charlie, 'unfasten your gunbelt.'

Devoid of any feasible alternative, Charlie obeyed. Under the gunman's guidance, he unbuckled the belt with his left hand, the discomfort of the wound ensuring his inability to make any quick, threatening movement. He held the belt by the buckle and when told to do so, threw it to the ground at his captor's feet.

Holding the pistol steady, its barrel pointed unwaveringly at Charlie's chest, the gunman bent his knees and gathered up the belt and holstered weapon. His dark eyes were fixed on Charlie, dull but watchful, almost as though he was the one being threatened and not the one with the advantage. Then, unexpectedly, he tossed away the pistol he was holding and began removing Charlie's Colt from its holster.

In that moment, Charlie knew he was about to be killed. The glint of murder flashed in the man's eyes. It was instantly clear to Charlie that the only reason he was not already dead was because the shot that had wounded him had been the man's last bullet. A glance at the man's waist confirmed that the loops of his cartridge belt were empty. Automatically, Charlie prepared to launch himself at his assailant, every muscle in his body tightened, but in the same instant that his instinct dictated an attack, his brain told him he had no hope of success. By the time he had covered the ground between them, the gun would be clear of leather and on this occasion the man would not fail to kill him.

Then fate took an unexpected hand. So anxious had the man been to replace his empty weapon with Charlie's loaded Colt that he had discarded it with a snarl of contempt. It looped over his shoulder and struck the rump of the red gelding whose lead rein was still wrapped around his left wrist. The nervy animal snorted and reared, swinging in front of the gunman, jerking him off balance and forming a barricade between him and Charlie. The man cursed as he staggered then yelled at the horse in the hope that it would remain still long enough for him to get a shot at Charlie Jefferson, but by the time a chance offered itself Charlie had disappeared.

Charlie Jefferson wasn't a coward but nor was he reckless with his life. He knew that the current mêlée caused by the skittered horse presented him with an opportunity to attack his ambusher, but the chances of success were not in his favour. While he remained an open target, his adversary needed only a moment to drill him with a bullet from his own gun. He would never regain possession of his horse and gun if he was dead. Instantly, he dashed towards the high boulders that edged the trail. Diving behind the nearest he found himself rolling into a long, narrow gully that seemed to run almost parallel with the road he had been following. At a stooped run, almost on hands and knees, he hurried along, hoping his manoeuvre would confuse the other man and that, unobserved, he would get behind him.

To his left Charlie could hear the sound of the man's struggle to control the still anxious animal. He paused a moment before raising his head above the edge of the gully. He was dismayed to find that his strategy had not rewarded him with any advantage. He had got himself into a position behind his enemy but the gap between them was, if anything, greater and the possibility of successfully rushing the man was even more remote.

The man had one foot in a stirrup, and although he still held the Colt in his hand Charlie had the impression he was content enough to have captured the horse, which provided the means for him to escape from this isolated place. With a string of angry words he swung into the saddle, the red gelding turning in its own length as he did so. As it turned the man caught sight of Charlie and instinctively threw a shot in his direction. A chunk of stone flew off a nearby boulder, causing Charlie to seek refuge again.

Keeping low, Charlie scrabbled along the gully expecting more bullets to be fired in his direction, but nothing came. The sound of hoofbeats reached him but they were not coming closer. When he risked another look, man and horse were a quarter of a mile away and very quickly extending that distance. Charlie stood and, gripped by a cold anger, he watched until they had disappeared from sight. He found the discarded, empty weapon and tucked it into the waistband of his trousers. He vowed to himself that it would be loaded when he caught up with the man who had robbed him and left him afoot on the vast prairie.

Unless the wound he'd received became infected and poisoned his system, Charlie knew that it was not fatal. Using his teeth and right hand he managed to wrap his neckerchief around his upper left arm and tie it tight in an attempt to stanch the loss of blood. Then he surveyed the Texas territory in which he had been marooned. It spread around him like an endless, flat carpet, but that was an illusion. This was an area of sudden troughs and surprising ridges, scrubland that was little better than a desert of dust and stones adorned here and there with scattered tufts of tough grass and tall cacti. Until the end of the war scrawny cattle had roamed free here, and Charlie remembered that, three years earlier, he and the Willis brothers had hoped to raise money by chasing some of those beasts down to the Arkansas timberland where beefsteaks were as rare as gold nuggets. But the brothers had been killed by a band of Southern bushwhackers who were still fighting the war three months after Lee's surrender at Appomattox. Those killings led to Charlie becoming a government agent and working secretly to destroy Rebel gangs in Arkansas, Missouri and Texas.

The danger involved in that work and the success he had achieved had earned him several bounties, enough money to fulfil the promise he'd made to Ruth Prescott the day he'd left his Wyoming home to fight in the war. Still little more than a youth, he and Ruth's brother, Amos, had headed east to enlist in the Union army, firm in the belief that the fighting would not last more than a few weeks. Seven years had passed since that day, years that had taken Amos's life and altered Charlie in many ways, but he remained true to his pledge to return to the valley of the Tatanka. There he would marry Ruth and build a ranch where they would raise the best beef cattle in the territory.

The bounty money he'd earned was in the form of four government indemnity bonds, and he'd hidden those bonds under the cloth lining of his saddle. It was an old, uncomfortable saddle, too unattractive for anyone to show interest in it or attempt to steal it. Unfortunately, the same couldn't be said for his horse, although if he'd been mounted on a jackass this day his unknown assailant would have taken it. So, despite the circumstances in which he found himself, Charlie's sole purpose as he set off across the inhospitable terrain was to regain his horse and money.

The three years he'd spent in the Union army

meant that he was no stranger to walking. He'd marched for hundreds of miles so the task before him wasn't immediately daunting, but he soon realized that high-heeled riding boots were unsuitable footwear for the journey. More than once he stumbled when he trod on loose rocks but all he could do was curse at his clumsiness and press on. The sun was high over his left shoulder, hot on his back despite his calico shirt. He scanned all around as he walked; he knew that since the war determined men had proclaimed ownership of vast tracts of this land and had seared their brand on every maverick they caught. Perhaps one of those men would be in this vicinity.

From the crest of each high point Charlie could see the swath cut by the red gelding's flight, but in the unchanging landscape it was difficult to assess how much ground he'd covered; he guessed it had been more than five miles. Then he became aware of the birds in the sky. Vultures were circling and swooping. At the top of the next rise he paused and studied them. About half a mile away several were gathered on the ground, feasting on a large, black form. Charlie guessed it was the thief's horse. The trail he was following led in that direction but he could see where, beyond the carcass, it swerved away to the left, which meant he could bypass the feeding scavengers and find the tracks again further south. He didn't like vultures and he didn't want to attract their attention. The thought of having them

12

following him didn't sit easily in his mind.

An hour later, footsore, dry-mouthed and damp with sweat, Charlie found himself on the lip of a deeper trough, a gulch through which, to his delight, ran a narrow stream. It was shallow, barely sufficient to cover the stones on the bed, but Charlie was able to refresh himself before resting awhile in the shade provided by the sheer, high bank. When he continued his trek he followed the course of the stream, figuring that as water was essential to support life it would be the surest way of finding a settlement.

The smell of smoke reached him less than an hour later. As he rounded a bend in the gulch he saw a low wooden building with a metal stovepipe sticking out of the roof. The smoke he could smell was climbing out of it into the sky. Beyond that first structure were two ramshackle outbuildings and at the side a dozen horses grazed within a well-constructed corral. Charlie blew out his cheeks with relief. If he could strike a quick bargain with the owner of those horses he might eat up a bit more of the thief's trail before nightfall.

CHAPTER TWO

Young Dave Champion caught sight of the movement along the gulch and thought it would be one of the white-tailed deer that sometimes drank there. He shifted his position on the top rail of the corral so that his back was wedged against the gatepost, then he blew once more into the high-pitched whistle, stopping and replaying a sequence when he made a mistake. When his gaze returned to the distant figure along the gulch he took the whistle from his lips and dropped to the ground. After one more look to confirm what he'd seen he hurried across to the house.

'Pa,' he said, 'someone's coming.' When that announcement didn't get a response he added, 'On foot.'

A few moments late, his father emerged from the building and side by side they observed the approaching stranger. Without comment they watched as the man made a detour to the corral,

14

and they exchanged only swift looks of curiosity when the dust-covered pilgrim stepped on to the bottom rail to get a good look at the animals in the enclosure. When that inspection was concluded, they waited motionless until the man stood before them.

'My horse was stolen,' Charlie Jefferson said, 'a big red gelding. Have you seen it?'

'You're the first person we've seen today,' Dave's father told him. 'When were you robbed?'

'Four, perhaps five hours ago.' Charlie looked over his shoulder. 'Must have covered fifteen miles,' he announced, 'perhaps more.'

'Better come inside,' Mr Champion said, 'I'll take a look at that arm and fix you some food.'

'I just want a horse and ammunition,' Charlie stated, 'and I'll pick up his trail again while there's still some daylight.'

The man indicated Charlie's left sleeve. 'You won't get anywhere if you don't get some repairs.'

Charlie knew the man was talking sense, was offering the sort of advice he would give to someone else in similar circumstances, but he was anxious to pursue his assailant. Not only had the man robbed him of his horse, weapons and money but without warning he had tried to kill him, then had left him to perish on the prairie. Charlie would not let those actions go unpunished.

But for now Mr Champion was ushering Charlie into the low building and telling his son to heat

15

some water with which to bathe the wound. There was little fresh blood now but, once the dried blood had been washed away, the open wound looked like a livid knife gash, as though some Shylock had begun taking his pound of flesh an ounce at a time. Champion packed the wound with a handful of flour before tying a patch of clean linen over it. On the battlefield Charlie had known medics use gunpowder in similar fashion to stanch blood loss. Sometimes it worked but sometimes it simply delayed the need for stitches.

Over a meal of stew and coffee, the man introduced himself as John Champion, superintendent of this relay station along the San Antonio - Santa Fe mail line. He and his son had lived out here for two years. It struck Charlie that this was an isolated spot for the lad, who was probably no more than fourteen years old, and he wasn't surprised when, after bringing him one of his father's shirts, young Davie loitered close at hand as though the presence of another human who wasn't just stepping out of a coach for a mug of coffee, was an exciting event.

Charlie gave an account of the ambush, describing the place where it happened and a description of his attacker. John Champion named the spot as Cleary's Canyon, but could offer no information that might identity the bushwhacker. In response to Charlie's query, he told him that Mortimer was the nearest settlement west of the relay station, a journey of twenty miles.

'It isn't much of a place,' John said. 'A gathering of old buildings that look like they'll collapse when the next tornado blows through, but the town councillors are determined to develop the place and make it an important town in Texas.'

'If my horse's tracks lead there, I'll find it,' declared Charlie. The tone of his voice left John Champion in no doubt that Charlie Jefferson was determined to seek vengeance. 'How much do you want for one of your horses?' Charlie asked.

'They aren't mine to sell,' John Champion told him. 'There's a stage through here tomorrow that'll take you to Mortimer. The driver will let you sit up top with him for free.'

Charlie shook his head. 'That's no good. I don't know for sure that the man I'm after was making for Mortimer. I need to pick up his trail tonight.' He explained how he'd quit following the tracks when he'd found the gulch, figuring he was more likely to find a settlement by following the water course than by wandering aimlessly across the prairie.

John Champion acknowledged the wisdom of that course of action; staying near water provided a better chance of survival, and Charlie's reaching this relay station had proved it, but he didn't agree that it was necessary to go hell for leather in pursuit of his assailant. If the tracks Charlie Jefferson had followed were heading west then his quarry's destination was almost certainly Mortimer; there was no other town for fifty miles around.

'Even if he isn't a citizen of Mortimer I reckon he'll find a bed there tonight. Chances are that he'll still be there when the stage rolls in tomorrow. I reckon he'll be surprised to see you, but even if he's moved on you'll be able to buy a fresh horse to continue your search.'

Charlie Jefferson weighed John Champion's advice against the dictates of his own conscience. There was much to be said for staying the night at the relay station. When he reached Mortimer it would be with a good meal under his belt and a night's sleep on something more comfortable than the stony Texas ground. Opposed to that, though, was the possibility that the man had not ridden towards Mortimer. According to John Champion it was a slim chance, but Charlie knew that if he lost the trail he was unlikely to find it again. He couldn't take the risk; if he didn't continue in pursuit of the man he might never see his horse or saddle again.

'What about settlers?' Charlie asked. 'Are there any farmers or cowmen around here?'

'One or two,' admitted John Champion, 'but none of them fit the description of the man you are looking for.'

'Perhaps he's a hired hand.'

'The only place big enough to employ men is Henry Sutton's place, but he didn't mention taking on any extra herders when he was here a couple of days ago.'

'Even so,' mused Charlie, 'the robber might have picked up some victuals there, then struck out in a different direction. I can't wait, Mr Champion. I can't afford to lose the trail.' He dipped his hand into a trouser pocket and brought out a handful of paper money: his travelling money which was meant to buy his necessary provisions on the way home. 'I need a horse and a box of ammunition,' he declared. 'That's all the money I have at present but if you'll trust me I'll make good any shortfall as soon as I get to the bank in Mortimer. I'll send the money out on the next stage heading this way.'

'Like I told you, Mr Jefferson, the horses aren't mine to sell. Heck, I'll give you the ammunition but I can't give you a horse.'

Charlie spread out the notes he'd dropped on the table. They didn't add up to a large sum. 'Tell you what,' he said, hoping that by adding something extra he'd be able to sway John Champion into parting with one of his animals, 'there's a dead horse a handful of miles back. I reckon it'll have a saddle that will be worth something and there might be a rifle there too. All you have to do is collect them.'

'It's not the money, Mr Jefferson,' said John Champion. 'It's my responsibility to make sure that there are enough well-rested horses to keep the coaches moving.'

The two men were at an impasse, each determined that his need was greater, yet both sympathetic to the other's predicament. It was John Champion who offered the compromise.

'I'll loan you a horse,' he said. 'You can take it as far as the Sutton spread. If the tracks don't lead to their place then the rider is sure to have gone into Mortimer. Strike a bargain with Henry Sutton for one of his saddle ponies. He or Sammy will be visiting in the next couple of days so one of them can bring back my horse.'

Although it was only half a solution to his problem, Charlie had to accept it was the best he would get. He didn't know how amenable Henry Sutton would be to parting with his livestock but Charlie would give it his best shot. He accepted the box of bullets that John Champion supplied and instantly loaded the revolver that his attacker had discarded.

Within minutes, they all rode away from the relay station, heading south where Charlie expected to find the tracks made by his big red gelding. Dave Champion was piping out a tune on his whistle as they rode and looked mighty pleased when he got to the end of the piece without needing to repeat a single sequence. Then he began again, but before he got too far into it Charlie spotted the kicked-up dirt he was seeking.

'He was riding hard,' declared Charlie as he pointed out the tracks of his stolen gelding. 'Either he was determined to put as much space between us as quickly as possible or he had some place to get to in a hurry.'

John Champion stood in his stirrups, gazing west as though it might still be possible to see the fleeing horse and rider. He was thinking that someone riding that fast had to be certain of the territory and his destination. This made him more convinced that the man planned to ride no further than Mortimer and that the sensible thing for Charlie Jefferson to do would be to rest up for the night, refresh himself and face the man in the morning. Instead, he said, 'Five miles ahead you'll find a south cut through some high ground. Follow that, it'll bring you to the Sutton spread.'

'I appreciate your help,' Charlie told him. 'I'll leave your horse with Mr Sutton.'

'Come on, Dave,' said his father as he swung his horse around to backtrack the fleeing robber, 'let's see what we can salvage from the dead horse.'

'Sure thing, Pa,' said the lad, but before kicking his heels against his pony's flanks he spoke to Charlie. 'Mr Jefferson, when you get to the Sutton place will you tell Sammy that I can already play Buffalo Gals?'

His father said, 'You call that playing?' but there was no malice in the remark.

Charlie promised to pass on the message and spurred his borrowed beast towards the west.

CHAPTER THREE

The horse under Charlie Jefferson had been bred
for stamina not speed, and Charlie had been wise
enough to handle it accordingly, asking no more
than a brisk canter of the animal. With its long
stride it had covered the distance to the collection
of boulders that led into the higher ground without
breaking sweat. Charlie had kept his eyes on the
ground ahead, watchful for any change of direction
by the man he was following, vigilant for any indication that he had quit his headlong flight and had
sought to avail himself of the high ground which
could provide a place to camp or an ambush point
for anyone on his trail.

But Charlie knew the man had no reason to
suspect that he was being followed; no reason to
suspect that the man he had robbed had any intention of retrieving his property. There was no
deviation to right or left, the trail was arrow straight,
heading, Charlie was now certain, for Mortimer.

The cut that led to the Sutton spread was identified by the imprint of iron-rimmed wheel tracks which were etched intermittently into the scuffed-up dust trail that had been formed by constant usage between there and Mortimer. Charlie Jefferson paused, knowing that that was the direction he was honour bound to take, but none the less he was tempted to keep on in pursuit of his property, figuring that the sooner he caught up with his quarry the greater the element of surprise would be. However, it was a brief moment of indecision and he cut south between the giant boulders. Before long he climbed a red-rock ridge, then dropped to a plateau where, widespread, cattle were grazing. To Charlie's eye the vegetation seemed little better than that of the scrubland over which he'd been travelling, but after a mile he reached a stream which flowed with more water than he had seen for several days, so he figured the grazing here would be superior to the coarse, sharp-bladed clumps he'd left behind.

He paused on the bank and allowed the horse to wet its lips and tongue while he swept the land ahead for signs of habitation. As though it was too lazy to climb higher, a cloud of dark smoke hung horizontally in the distant sky. Charlie figured that it would be coming from the home of the Suttons and he gee'd the horse across the stream in that direction. He didn't get far. A cry off to his left reached his ears and he pulled the horse to a halt.

Two horses, some distance apart, were watching him, their reins trailing as though their riders had left them to forage while they tended to their own business. Charlie turned in their direction, moving at walking pace because experience had taught him that some people reacted unpredictably when strangers came at them in a hurry. He scanned the area near the horses and, at first, couldn't see anyone, but suddenly, a dozen yards beyond the animals, a figure rose from the ground and waved an arm to attract his attention.

'Over here,' the girl called, and Charlie urged a quicker speed from his own mount.

'This man's hurt,' the girl said as Charlie stepped down to join her. At her feet a man lay on his back. One leg was bent at the knee and his arms were spread away from his body. His head was bare and blood, pumping from a fresh bullet wound, was darkening his blue shirt at an alarming rate.

Charlie's medical knowledge was limited but he had seen enough battlefield injuries to know that there was little hope of recovery for the man. A yellow bandanna had been applied to the wound in an effort to stanch the flow but it had been a futile gesture; it was smothered in blood and Charlie saw that the girl's hands, too, were covered in the man's gore.

Charlie looked the girl in the eye. 'He needs the attention of a proper doctor,' he told her, but the look she gave him in return made it clear that she knew as well as he did that even a proper physician couldn't save the man's life.

'The nearest one is in Mortimer,' she said, 'but I'll ride back to the house and get a wagon if you'll wait here.'

Charlie agreed and, after rubbing her hands dry on the ground, the girl ran to the waiting horses, climbed lithely on to the smaller one, a dappled filly, and set off at speed in the direction of the low-hanging smoke.

A moan dragged Charlie's attention back to the wounded man, who was moving his arms in an awkward fashion. Charlie found a water canteen on the saddle of the man's horse and poured a few drops on to his lips. His eyelids flickered and when they opened they revealed watery eyes of fading blue which struggled to retain any focus. His lips moved, as though needing to speak, but the effort required was too great and once again his eyes closed and his head grew heavy against Charlie's arm.

'Take it easy,' Charlie murmured, 'help is on its way.'

The sound of the voice rekindled the man's effort. His right hand gripped Charlie's arm and his eyes reopened. This time they held a dull light as though he recognized the face before him. With a glint of determination he reached up with his left hand to grip the front of Charlie's shirt.

'Farraday,' he said, and the grimace that followed

was testament to the toll demanded for the utterance of that one word. None the less, when his eyes reopened, he spoke again. 'Be careful, Tom.'

Any thought that Charlie had of denying that his name was Tom was never uttered; there didn't seem to be any point because he was sure that the man wasn't in any condition to understand him. If he wanted to believe he was talking to someone called Tom then, under the circumstances, what did it matter? But now the man's hand had released its grip on the front of Charlie's shirt and was struggling to undo the button on the pocket of his own shirt. After a moment or two Charlie assisted and withdrew a somewhat bloodied, folded document.

'Take it,' murmured the man. Although his voice was weak, his strength swiftly ebbing, Charlie sensed that the paper was important. When he unfolded and read the bloodied document, it revealed that Clem Cole was a Texas Ranger. Wrapped inside was a metal badge of office. He wondered if Tom, too, was a Ranger and where he could be found, but when he returned his attention to Clem Cole it was clear that he wouldn't be able to supply that information. Clem Cole had died in the line of duty.

Some minutes later a buckboard, throwing up dust and rattling like the medicine bones of a Sioux holy man, hove into view. The driver was yelling and flapping the reins like all the devils of hell were on his tail, but his only companion was the girl on the dappled filly. He yanked the horses to an abrupt halt and the back of the wagon slewed a little way to the left before rocking to a halt. The man applied the brake, reached for a bag on the seat at his side, then leapt to the ground. Hurrying across to the gunshot victim he barely spared a glance for Charlie, but when he looked down the urgency that had until that moment been evident, dissipated like snow subjected to sudden heat.

'Too late,' he said, speaking to the girl who had dismounted and now stood at his side, 'but with that wound I couldn't have done anything to save him. Do you know him?'

'I've seen him around town recently. He might have found work at Mr Gowland's store.'

The man's grunt expressed the view that selling goods and stacking shelves wasn't suitable work for a man but he didn't put it into words and he fixed his attention on Charlie Jefferson. 'A friend of yours?' he asked and when Charlie shook his head he followed with two more questions. 'Who are you and what are you doing here?'

The abrupt tone didn't sit easy with Charlie but he was prepared to attribute it to the violent death, in such circumstances men's reactions were often against their nature. 'I have business with Mr Sutton.'

'He's not hiring,' the man said.

'Buck,' said the girl, 'the sheriff will have to investigate the killing. Why don't you take the body into town. Perhaps,' she said to Charlie, 'you'll give him a hand to get it on the wagon, Mr ... er. . . ?'

'Jefferson, miss. Charlie Jefferson.' He bent to grab the legs of the cadaver and hoist it on to the long flatboards of the wagon.

Buck seemed less than eager to leave the girl alone in the company of the stranger, making it clear by his grim-faced expression that he had no reason to suppose that Charlie Jefferson wasn't the perpetrator of the recent killing, but the girl dismissed him with a grin; she, Charlie realized, carried the greater authority. Casually, he studied her, estimated she was no more than twenty years of age, but the assurance of her manner belied her youth. She sat straight and proud in the saddle and as they rode off in the opposite direction to Buck and the wagon, she asked him what business he had with her father. Unsurprised by the fact that she was Henry Sutton's daughter he explained the situation; how the horse he was now astride needed to be returned to the relay station and that he hoped to replace it with one of her father's.

'I'm sure we'll have something suitable,' she told him.

It was a short ride to the compound where a collection of wooden buildings acted as home for the Sutton family with a bunkhouse for the hired men, barns for the animals and stores for fodder and equipment. The girl led the way to the main building where a thickset, middle-aged man with greying hair stood on the veranda. This was Henry Sutton, who listened carefully to his daughter's report but rarely shifted his gaze from the tall stranger who sat his horse alongside the girl.

'I sent Buck into town with the body,' the girl concluded. 'I suppose Sheriff Agnew will be coming out to investigate.'

Henry Sutton nodded his approval and turned his attention to Charlie Jefferson, wanting to know what part he'd played in the recent events and why he was on Sutton range. Once again Charlie told his story, which included a detailed description of his attacker. The cattleman listened attentively but neither he nor his daughter could put a name to the man who had taken Charlie's horse. The matter of a replacement horse to get him as far as Mortimer was resolved in like manner to that envisaged by John Champion. Charlie had proved himself honest by arriving at the ranch with the relay horse so Henry Sutton was prepared to provide one which could be left for collection at the livery stable.

'All our stock is branded,' the rancher announced. 'Gus Brewer will see that it gets back here and no doubt he'll have an animal you can buy.'

Those words seemed to end Henry Sutton's interest in Charlie Jefferson but, still remembering Clem Cole's dying words, Charlie delayed his departure by asking a question. 'Is the name Farraday familiar to you?'

The cattleman considered for a moment then shook his head. His daughter, too, declared that she knew no one of that name. Charlie told them that that had been the name on the dying man's lips; perhaps it was the name of his killer, although he had to admit that the man had been confused because he thought he was talking to someone called Tom.

'I'll ask the crew,' Henry Sutton told him. 'They know more people in Mortimer. At least it's a clue for the sheriff to follow.'

Those hands who were within yelling distance were summoned. When they'd gathered at the foot of the veranda they were addressed by their boss.

'A man's been killed a short distance from the house,' he announced, 'a stranger to me, a newcomer to Mortimer, possibly working at Gowland's store. Does anyone know him?'

Charlie watched the group of men and when one of them threw out the name Harv Johnson it raised murmurs of agreement from a couple of those assembled. The fact that he hadn't used the name Clem Cole suggested to Charlie that the dead man had been working on an under-cover assignment. He was pleased he hadn't shown the badge and document to anyone; he would give that information to the sheriff.

Charlie addressed the cowboy who had provided the name. 'Did Harv have any particular friends in town? Perhaps someone called Tom? He was confused at the end, thought I was someone called Tom.'

The cowboy shook his head, reluctant to offer anything to a stranger as was the way in such an isolated community. A couple of the men kept their eyes fixed on Charlie but no one spoke.

'How about the name Farraday?' asked Henry Sutton. 'Any of you know a fellow by that name?'

There was head-shaking, men looking at each other to assure themselves that their ignorance was in keeping with that of the rest of the crew, and murmurs of 'No, boss,' to prove to Charlie that their loyalty was to the man who paid for their time.

At the back of the group a moustachioed man, not much older than Charlie, had his head bowed as he concentrated on freeing a rock from the ground with his foot. He wore a red plaid shirt and leather chaps over black trousers. When he raised his head his glance went first to Charlie; then when he realized that he was under observation he turned away as if to speak to his neighbour.

Henry Sutton dismissed the men and after promising to give the information to the sheriff when he showed up, indicated to Charlie the way to the stables.

'There'll be somebody hanging around there,' he said. 'They'll find a suitable swap for that horse of Champion's.'

'I'll go with Mr Jefferson,' said his daughter, and she turned the head of the dappled filly off in the direction of the stables.

'Won't you stay and take a meal with us, Mr Jefferson?'

'Kind of you, miss, but I want to get to Mortimer as soon as possible.'

'Do you think the man who stole your horse will still be there?'

'I do.'

The iciness in Charlie's voice didn't invite an extension of that conversation so they rode to the stable in silence. Charlie hadn't intended rudeness but he was aware that his abrupt response had taken the girl by surprise. As they unsaddled he recalled a promise he'd made earlier in the day and hoped that the change of subject would remove the roughness from his manner.

'I have a message for your younger brother.'

The girl gave him a quizzical look. 'I don't have a younger brother. I don't have a brother of any age.'

'I must have misunderstood,' apologized Charlie, 'when Dave spoke about Sammy I got the impression he was Mr Sutton's son.'

The girl laughed. 'She's Mr Sutton's daughter,' she told him. 'I'm Sammy. Samantha. You are not the first one to make that mistake.'

'Are you the one who gave young Dave the whistle?'

'Yes. He's isolated out at that relay station so I ride over at least once a week to break the monotony. Sometimes I take books to make sure he doesn't forget how to read and write, but last time I thought something musical might interest him.'

'I have to tell you that already he can play *Buffalo Gals.*'

Sammy Sutton raised her eyebrows in admiration of her young friend's achievement; Charlie hadn't the heart to tell her that Dave's father's opinion was less favourable.

Sammy Sutton stayed with Charlie while he selected a dun mare, saddled it and climbed on to its back. 'I'll leave horse and tack at the livery,' he promised.

She wanted to tell him that she hoped he found his horse but kept the thought to herself. When he did there would be violence and she'd seen enough of that for one day.

'We'll be pleased to see you if you come back this way,' she said, 'and I'll insist that you sit at table with us.'

Charlie was amused by the girl's words because her father hadn't given any indication that he would be pleased to see him again but, regardless of that, when he recovered his property he intended heading north to his home in Wyoming. But Sammy was being hospitable and he had no reason to be anything but polite to her. He smiled, as though her invitation was a source of great pleasure, and was rewarded by the sight of Sammy's face brightening in response; he figured that it was time for her to shed the tomboy name. He tipped his hat, put heels to the horse and rode away towards Mortimer.

He'd covered less than twenty yards before reining in the mount. Three riders, moving at walking pace, were heading in his direction. All the men were strangers to Charlie, two of them typical scrawny cattle herders, toughened by the conditions in which they worked, but it was the man in the middle who had captured Charlie's attention. He was a lanky cowboy, younger than his companions, with his hat pushed to the back of his head to reveal straw-coloured hair. Charlie turned his horse across the line of their approach, his right hand resting lightly on his thigh close to the revolver tucked into the waistband of his trousers. His eyes were fixed on the trio, watching for a reaction to his manoeuvre.

The conversation between the approaching riders ended, their faces were etched with expressions of curiosity. 'Something we can do for you?' asked the oldest rider, the one on the right.

Charlie spoke to the man in the middle. 'You can tell me what you're doing on my horse.'

CHAPTER FOUR

Sammy Sutton eased the tension caused by Charlie's aggressive confrontation. Eager to learn the reason for delaying his departure she had followed in his wake and had been close enough to hear the question he'd asked. A swift glance was enough to confirm that the big red gelding being ridden by Eli Ringwood had not been picked that morning from the Sutton corral.

'Where did you get him, Eli?' Sammy's voice was a settling influence, an assurance to the cow-hands that they had her support in any argument.

'Came across an hombre earlier who had run this fellow almost to exhaustion,' said the lanky cowboy. 'He told us he was in a hurry to get to Mortimer and needed to change horses. I was riding old Job so we figured it was a good deal. Job would get the fellow to where he was going and we got this fine gelding. He might not work cattle as well as Job but he's younger and I'll wager he'll be a mighty fine travelling horse when he's rested up.'

Charlie stepped down from his saddle to examine the red. It stood quietly while the familiar hand rubbed its nose and neck. There were marks on its hindquarters where it had been lashed with the leathers. Charlie looked up at the rider.

'We saw them,' said Eli Ringwood, 'but the man had told us he was in a hurry. Whatever reason he had for reaching Mortimer must have been important.'

Charlie asked for a description of the man and it tallied with that of the man who had tried to kill him out in the wilderness. 'Is that your own saddle?' he asked.

'Sure,' answered Eli. 'A man doesn't part with his work equipment.'

'Miss,' Charlie switched his attention to Sammy Sutton, 'I'll be wanting my horse back.'

'He's in no condition to travel any more today,' she said.

'He's Sutton stock now,' announced one of the older cowboys, tetchy because they'd only acquired the superior red by trading what hadn't been theirs to trade.'

Charlie didn't argue but spoke to the girl again. 'I'd be obliged if you didn't put a brand on him before I return.' Swiftly he remounted and departed, the horse settling into a steady canter as it ate into the miles that separated the Sutton ranch from Mortimer.

*

The lowest rim of the sun was already hidden by the western hills when Charlie reached Mortimer. Shadows were long and Charlie reckoned that the last of that day's sunlight would be gone in less than an hour. The business part of town was compact and matched John Champion's description. Offices, saloons and stores were old timber buildings gathered close together along both sides of a dusty street, but the sounds of construction work and the smell of fresh timber carried to him from behind the buildings to his right, a sign that in the aftermath of the war this town was beginning to grow.

The men and women walking the boardwalks were going about their business with civic politeness and few took any notice of Charlie's entrance into their town. Charlie inspected all the tethered horses along the street but none carried the Sutton brand nor, more importantly, his old saddle. Two-thirds of the way along the street Charlie spotted the buckboard that had been used to transport the dead Texas Ranger from the Sutton ranch. It stood outside a high-fronted, whitewashed building and as he got closer, he could read the name on the board fixed over the door: George Weightman, Carpenter. Charlie figured that George Weightman built coffins. He was about to ride past and seek out the livery to stable the horse before finding a room for himself, but at that moment two men came out

37

of the carpenter's shop, one of whom he recognized.

'That's the fella,' said Buck, the wary cowboy who had brought Clem Cole's body to town.

His companion was a broad-shouldered man of average height. He wore black trousers, a black waistcoat over a plain blue plaid shirt and from beneath his black hat silver hair showed. But he wasn't an old man, no more than fifty, and his movements were quick and vigorous. A metal badge was fastened to the pocket of his waistcoat to announce the position he held in Mortimer.

'Wait up, young fella,' he called to Charlie and raised his arm to emphasize the command.

Charlie turned the horse towards the boardwalk and dropped his hands on to the saddle horn when it came to a halt. 'I was coming to see you after I'd stabled the horse,' Charlie announced. He'd expected to meet the sheriff on the trail, figuring the lawman would have responded swiftly to news of a sudden death.

'Buck tells me that you were in the vicinity when Harv Johnson got shot.'

'Well, Buck's got it wrong. I was with the man when he died. I don't know where or how long before that he was shot. It was Miss Sutton who came across him first. I responded to her call for assistance.'

The sheriff threw a look at Buck as though expecting those facts to be contested but when it became clear that the old cowboy had no argument to offer he told him to head back to the ranch.

'Tell Sammy I'll need a statement from her,' he added, 'I expect she'll be coming to town tomorrow with Henry. He'll want his say at the meeting.'

'Aren't you going out there to investigate, Sheriff?' Charlie asked.

'Sure I am, but there's nothing I can do today,' the lawman replied. 'It'll soon be too dark to see anything. Tomorrow I need to be in town for the meeting, so I'll hear what Sammy has to say when she gets here.'

'I reckon it was murder, Sheriff. Doesn't that justify a bit more urgency on your part?'

The sheriff squinted a steely look at Charlie. 'First off,' he said, 'being sheriff of Mortimer doesn't give me any authority over the sun. I can't prevent it dropping behind those hills no matter what crime has been committed. And second, I don't need any advice on how to do my job from a dust-covered drifter. Now, if you'll get down from that animal, we'll walk across the street to my office and I'll hear your story.'

Sheriff Abe Agnew stuck his unlit pipe in his mouth and leant back in his rounded desk chair while he listened to Charlie's account of the happenings since he'd been shot at and robbed out in the eastern scrubland. Charlie concluded by handing over the documents that the dead man had been carrying.

'A Texas Ranger,' muttered Sheriff Agnew. 'A telegraph message to their headquarters in Austin will quickly confirm if these papers are genuine.'

'Perhaps the reply will provide some means of identifying this fellow Farraday. Even though he was dying, Johnson or Cole or whatever his name was seemed determined to pass on the information that Farraday was his slayer.'

'In my experience, the Rangers keep their cards close to their chest. They'll only tell me what I need to know.'

Charlie moved towards the door. 'If you are done with me I'll go and stable my horse.'

'Are you planning to stay around town?'

'I intend to find the man who robbed me and tried to kill me.'

'And when you do?'

'I guess that's up to him. If he's the cooperative kind I'll bring him to you so that the law can punish him.'

'And if he isn't?'

'I reckon Mr Weightman will have to construct a wooden box for either him or me.'

'Jefferson, this town has big plans. Lawless behaviour won't be tolerated.'

'Unless the sun has dropped behind the hills, Sheriff.'

Charlie didn't give Abe Agnew the opportunity to respond to the slight he had thrown in his direction. He left the office, untied his horse from the rail outside and rode further along the street to the livery. He dismounted out front and led the Sutton horse into the dark, high, timber-built structure.

Beyond the rear doors Gus Brewer, the stableman, left the dun-coloured mare he had been running a curry comb over, and greeted Charlie.

'Are you a new hand at the Sutton spread?' His eyes had lingered for a moment on the brand burned high on the haunch of Charlie's horse.

'No, just borrowed one of their horses for a day or two.'

With a look at Charlie that was charged with suspicion, Gus Brewer took the reins and led the horse into a stall.

'Something wrong?' asked Charlie.

'I don't know,' replied the stableman, 'but when two Sutton horses arrive in town carrying strangers on the same day it seems that something strange is happening out at Henry's place. He's not a man easily parted from his property.'

'You've got another Sutton horse stabled here?'

'Sure do.'

'Would it be a horse you recognize? A horse called Job?'

'That's the one,' confirmed Gus Brewer. 'He's out in the corral.'

'Do you know the man who brought him in?'

'Like I said,' Gus answered as he loosened the girth strap to lift the saddle from the dun mare, 'you're the second stranger on a Sutton horse today.'

41

'Did he give a name?'

'Harker.' Before Charlie could pose another question the stableman spoke again. 'Don't know his business, nor where he went from here. If he'd asked my advice I'd've told him to find a room that supplied hot water because it was clear he'd been travelling hard and was in need of a bath. But there's an abundance of hotels in Mortimer and I don't know which one he chose.'

'Did he leave his saddle here?' asked Charlie.

Gus nodded and indicated the long rail behind Charlie. 'That's it on the end.'

Charlie swung around, his eyes sweeping over four harness sets that straddled the rail. The end saddle was dark, almost black and had borne someone for many miles, but that someone hadn't been Charlie. Although the rig wasn't new, it wasn't the old one into which Charlie had sewn his wealth. It needed only the briefest glance to dispel any thought that the stableman's memory had failed him and that his saddle was in a different position on the rail. Now it was essential to find the man who had robbed him if he was ever to recover his money.

At that moment the man called Harker had his dusty trousers planted on a chair in one of the finest suites of the Hotel of the Republic on Houston Street. It was a grand name for a modest building with only eight rooms available for travellers, but it had been in existence since before Sam Houston's

Texans had triumphed over the Mexican force of General Santa Anna at the Battle of San Jacinto, and in celebration of that victory successive owners had ensured that its size had not limited the splendour of its interior.

Hunger gripped at Harker's stomach and he wanted nothing more than to fill it with food, then find a bed on which to stretch his travel-weary body, but his headlong flight had not been without purpose: delivering his news to the occupant of this suite had been his first priority. Two other men were present. One, dressed in dark range clothes, was long and lean. His shoulders rested against the wall, his arms were crossed and his chin almost touched his chest, as though boredom had brought on sleep. It was a stance that had fooled many men in the past and if they had taken notice of the double gunbelt that encircled his waist, its holsters secured low on his thighs by leather strings, they would surely have known that this was a dangerous man to underestimate. Even now, although displaying indifference to Harker's words, he listened intently.

The third man was sitting on a long settee. He was a big man, wearing a white linen shirt with a silver-coloured silk cravat below the jacket of his fashionable suit. From time to time he drew on the half-smoked cigar that was gripped in his left hand. When he spoke his voice held a hint of amusement, which surprised Harker.

'Texas Rangers.' The man tapped ash into a dish.

'Who are they looking for?'

Harker's voice betrayed his surprise at the question. 'You and me.'

'Me? Thomas Cartwright? Is it not Courtney Farraday that they want?'

'Of course, but using a different name isn't foolproof. They have a good description of you. You were seen by a lot of people in Johnson City and if the Rangers get a hint that the same scheme is being pulled here they'll soon be swarming all over Mortimer.'

Thomas Cartwright nodded as though accepting Harker's argument. 'Dangerous people to mess with, those Rangers,' he said. 'What do you think, Sol?'

The tall man leaning against the wall raised his head. 'Wasn't that dangerous,' he said. 'One shot was all it took.' He dropped his head on to his chest again.

Harker looked from Sol Barclay to Thomas Cartwright, understanding slowly dawning. 'You've already tangled with the Rangers?'

'Tangled with and disposed of,' crowed Cartwright. 'Sol became suspicious of a nosy store clerk and intercepted a telegraph message intended for Austin. The store clerk was a Texas Ranger. He met with an accident earlier today.'

Harker cast a glance towards Sol Barclay but the gunman didn't raise his head. 'Then we need to get away from this place as quickly as possible.'

Cartwright grinned and raised a hand to placate Harker. 'Oh, we'll leave shortly but not before we've filled our pockets. The store clerk's message didn't get sent to Austin so we still have time on our side. There's a meeting tomorrow. I'll get all the money they've raised and we'll be out of Mortimer before nightfall.'

Harker was alarmed by the other's nonchalance. He had barely escaped with his life after being recognized by a pair of Texas Rangers who had chased him for miles into the scrubland. He still wasn't sure how he'd escaped their guns even though his horse had been mortally wounded in the running gunfight and he'd almost exhausted his ammunition. But the horse had run on long enough for him to avoid capture and he'd made his way to Mortimer to warn his partner that Rangers were scattered across the territory in order to apprehend those involved in the Johnson City swindle. In his opinion they ought to quit the state and divide up the money they had so far amassed. But now it appeared that the man he still thought of as Courtney Farraday believed that he could outwit these townspeople and the Texas Rangers.

'Perhaps the store clerk isn't the only Texas Ranger here in Mortimer,' he said.

'Relax,' said Farraday. 'Even if he had a partner it's possible that his body won't be found before tomorrow's meeting. In three days we'll be rich and in New Mexico. Go and get something to eat, a night's sleep and we'll meet at the courthouse in the morning.'

CHAPTER FIVE

In order to establish the persona of a man of wealth and influence, it had been essential for Courtney Farraday, aka Thomas Cartwright, to take rooms at the Hotel of the Republic, but his partner, Harker, was more accustomed to rough living and the grandeur with which Farraday liked to be surrounded held no appeal for him. So he left the hotel and headed down the street, attracted by the usual raucous sounds of night-time activities in a frontier town.

His immediate needs were filled at the Rose of Texas. In addition to acquiring a key for one of the upstairs bedrooms he was served a huge plateful of stew, which he washed down with a cold beer. With food and drink in his belly the weariness of the day became less oppressive, and when a songstress in silks and feathers sashayed her musical way between tables he knew he would be propping up the bar long into the night. The girl's voice was unexceptional but she had other attributes that pleased those assembled in the long room and at the end of her performance Harker wasn't the only man anxious to claim her attention. Although she smiled at each of them she tarried with none and quit the room via a door behind the pianist.

Harker lingered at the bar, talking to no one but listening to the scraps of conversation that carried in his direction. More than one person spoke of the meeting due to be held next day in the courthouse. It had been announced that the town council would be making a proposal that would benefit Mortimer, but no one seemed to have any knowledge of what that proposal would be. Most people were prepared to write it off as another pipe dream of the mayor, Dustin Baker, who, apparently, was not held in any especial esteem, for more than one joke was passed at his expense. In a few days' time, Harker thought, if all went well with the scheme, few people would be laughing in Mortimer.

A general pandemonium in the room meant that Harker had little chance of sleep in his bedroom above, so he dropped a coin on the counter for the barman to refill his whiskey glass. It was at that moment that he felt the hand on his shoulder and was pushed roughly along the bar so that he collided with the two nearest patrons. In the ensuing confusion, glasses were sent crashing to the floor and Harker stumbled, eventually coming to a halt on one knee beside a nearby gaming table. He cursed, his hand sought the butt of the pistol at his side and he looked up, ready to challenge whoever had caused the indignity.

'Go ahead,' said Charlie Jefferson, looking down on the man he had ridden into Mortimer to find. 'Pull that gun and I'll plug you as you deserve.'

It took a moment for Harker to recognize the man he'd robbed and left to perish in the distant scrubland, and his surprise that the man had reached Mortimer so quickly was scored in his expression.

Around the room men were getting to their feet, pushing forward to get closer to the incident, curious to know the cause of the disturbance, anxious to witness at first hand whatever ensued.

Charlie Jefferson held his hands above waist height, allowing everyone to see that he was prepared to give the man on the floor an even chance.

'This man ambushed me, stole my horse and gun and left me to die.'

Many eyes turned towards Harker, waiting for his version of events, waiting to see if he would try to fight his way out of the situation. No one liked a horse-thief especially one who left the owner afoot in isolated territory. But Harker remained silent, his eyes narrowing to watch for any sudden movement by his accuser.

'That's my gun at your side,' said Charlie. 'You can either try to use it or you can come with me to the sheriff's office, but first you're going to tell me what you've done with my saddle.'

Harker swallowed; he was no stranger to gunplay but it was rarely face to face, unless he had an edge. But there was an implication in his opponent's final words that he wasn't yet prepared to shoot. Perhaps that was the advantage he needed. Suddenly his hand gripped the pistol butt and began to pull the weapon free of its holster, but just as suddenly as he had made his move he stopped again. He was looking into the barrel of Charlie Jefferson's gun with the hammer fully cocked under his thumb. Harker's eyes widened and sweat showed on his face.

'No man would blame me if I let this hammer fall,' said Charlie, his voice low, laden with the promise of death for Harker.

'I would.' The words came from behind Charlie and were accompanied by the pressure of a gun barrel in his back. 'Ease off the hammer and hand that gun to me.'

Charlie recognized the voice. Sheriff Abe Agnew, he figured, had followed him from his office and was determined to keep order in his town. He passed his gun to the sheriff, who was making the same demand of Harker.

'That's my gun,' Charlie explained, 'the one he stole when he ambushed me.'

'We'll sort that out down at my office,' the lawman said. He motioned for both men to precede him out of the saloon.

On the street their progress towards the sheriff's office was watched with interest by a handful of citizens. Among them, keeping to the darkness of the boardwalk, was a man dressed in black who had recently quit a room in the Hotel of the Republic. When the sheriff and his prisoners reached their destination, Sol Barclay retraced his steps to report to Thomas Cartwright.

Charlie Jefferson talked all the way to the jail, recounting once more details of the ambush and insisting that the other man under the sheriff's gun had robbed him and attempted to kill him.

'You've got no proof of that,' said Harker as they entered the sheriff's office.

'You've still got my gunbelt around your waist,' declared Charlie.

Harker had no reply but he doubted whether Charlie could prove that either gunbelt or gun was his property.

Sheriff Agnew picked up a ring of keys from his desk and herded the men towards the cells.

Charlie protested. 'What are you doing, Sheriff? He's the criminal.'

'I'm locking up both of you. Tomorrow, or perhaps the day after, the judge will listen to your complaint. If he believes your story then this one will be punished, and if he doesn't then you'll be charged with disturbing the peace and threatening behaviour.'

'You can't do that, Sheriff.'

'Sure I can. Can you prove your story?'

After a moment's thought, Charlie nodded his head. 'Do you know a lanky cowboy called Eli who works for Henry Sutton?'

'I know him.'

'He's got my horse, swapped it with this fellow for the Sutton horse he rode into Mortimer.'

'You were on a Sutton horse yourself when you came to town and I'm not forgetting that you were out at the Sutton place when the store clerk got killed.'

Charlie thought that surrendering the Texas Ranger's identification had already cleared him from suspicion of that crime.

'I'm sure Henry Sutton and his daughter will vouch for me and Eli will identify this man as the one who gave him my red gelding.'

'I expect Henry will be in town tomorrow. I'll speak to him. If he confirms your story you'll get out of here and then, I hope, you'll ride clear of Mortimer.' With those words he locked his prisoners in separate cells, tossed the keys on to his desk and set about brewing a pot of coffee on the pot-bellied stove in the corner.

Frustrated by his imprisonment, Charlie Jefferson grumbled at the lawman until eventually, weary of hearing Charlie's voice, the sheriff turned out the lamps and closed the door that separated the cells from his office. Knowing that he was unlikely to regain the sheriff's attention before morning, Charlie lay on his bunk and hoped that sleep would claim him. It didn't come because the close proximity of the man who had bushwhacked him kept his mind active: he was anxious to have him reveal what he'd done with his old saddle, but when he asked the question his fellow prisoner refused to answer.

Eventually, despite the discomfort of the bunk and the wheezes, grunts and snores in the outer office, the rigours of the day took their toll and Charlie fell asleep, but it seemed as though his eyes had been closed for only a few moments when a noise forced him to open them again.

The disturbance was caused by a voice, not strident but husky and calling with urgent secrecy from beyond the cells. When it wasn't instantly repeated Charlie wondered if it had been a figment of his imagination, but he dismissed that thought moments later when the call came again.

'Harker.'

Unsure if Harker had heard the call, Charlie moved slowly in the darkness, turning only his head to watch for movement in the adjoining cell. There was no movement and the noises of sleep from the outer office continued. The call came again, low and soft but urgent and this time it was accompanied by a light, metallic ring. Charlie knew the source of the sound. High on the rear wall of each cell was a two-barred opening and someone had taken up a position outside Harker's cell.

The last call had aroused Harker. Swiftly, sure that the darkness obscured his movement, he stood on his bunk so that his head was level with the opening. Outside, Sol Barclay had clambered on to a discarded barrel which he'd rolled into position and now the two met face to face.

'What are you doing in there?' asked Barclay. He'd been commissioned by Cartwright with the task of learning the reason for Harker's arrest and, if necessary, to determine a means of getting him out of jail. Cartwright had had no reason to suppose that his partner's arrest was in connection with the swindle but he wasn't prepared to take any chances; nothing must interfere with the scheme now that it was close to its conclusion.

Concerned that he might awaken Charlie Jefferson or be interrupted by the sheriff, Harker explained the situation to Sol Barclay.

'If the cowboy I swapped horses with comes to town he'll confirm Jefferson's story. You've got to get me out of here. Soon.'

With a nod of his head, a gesture indicating that something would be done to get Harker out of his current predicament, Barclay moved away from the bars in preparation to jump down to the ground. But the prisoner called to him once more, his voice louder as he stressed the urgency of his need.

'Something has to be done,' he said. 'Tell Farraday to get me out of here quickly.'

'Farraday!' Charlie Jefferson's yell reverberated in the cells. Alerted by the name that had been uttered by the dying Texas Ranger, Charlie had jumped to his feet and was now calling out to get the attention of Sheriff Agnew.

Harker, still grasping the bars of the aperture, turned his head at the sound of Charlie's shout. He didn't know why Farraday's name should elicit such a response from his fellow prisoner but he knew it didn't augur well for the success of their scheme. His anxiety at the possibility of being proved a horse-thief was increased by the new turn of events and he threw an appeal at Sol Barclay.

'Do something.'

Barclay had been thinking along the same lines. He knew that the Texas Rangers were hunting for a man called Farraday; he couldn't allow the hue and cry to concentrate on this town at this time. He did something. He drew his gun and shot Harker in the head, the body falling heavily to the floor.

The gunshot put an abrupt end to Charlie's shouting. Another shot was fired, aimed from the high aperture into Charlie's cell. The lump of lead clanged against the long bars beside which he was standing and ricocheted into a wall. Charlie rolled across the floor towards the back wall, hoping that the darkness and the angle created would make it impossible for the gunman to hit him. It did but, none the less, the attacker fired two more shots which became embedded in the planks of the floor.

Sheriff Agnew, startled from his snores, reacted swiftly and was at the cells with gun in hand in a matter of moments. But the gunman had now fled from his perch outside the jailhouse and all that remained for the lawman to do was to fetch a lamp and examine the outcome of the attack.

The bullet in the forehead had killed Harker instantly.

'I don't suppose you saw his killer,' said the sheriff.

'Too dark,' admitted Charlie.

The sheriff grimaced. 'I'll take a look around the back, perhaps there'll be some marks that will identify him.'

'What about me, Sheriff? Do you believe my story now? How about releasing me? It might not be safe for me here. The killer might come back for me. He was anxious enough to put lead in me a few minutes ago.'

'If Henry Sutton vouches for you I'll set you free. If you didn't steal that Sutton horse then you'll only be here a few more hours.'

'Sheriff, would I have brought him to Mortimer if I'd stolen him? And Buck has already confirmed that I was at the Sutton spread.'

But Sheriff Agnew wasn't to be swayed; until he was sure of the facts Charlie Jefferson would stay in jail.

When the sheriff left Charlie regarded the body on the floor in the next cell. Sheriff Agnew had thrown a blanket over the dead man and there was a bloodstain where the hole in his head had been made.

'Where's my saddle?' asked Charlie, but he knew he would probably never get an answer to that question now.

CHAPTER SIX

'You killed him?'

Harker and Thomas Cartwright had been part-
ners for several years and there was no hint of anger
in the latter's voice, merely a question as to whether
or not the right course of action had been taken.
Cartwright continued eating the breakfast that had
been delivered to his room before Sol Barclay's
arrival.

'You said to deal with the situation. If I'd left him
in jail the sheriff would have wanted to know where
to find Farraday.'

'Harker might have kept quiet.'

'I didn't think it was worth the risk.'

Cartwright grunted, probably in agreement with
Barclay. 'What about the other fellow?' he asked.

'I don't think I hit him. It was too dark to get a
good shot and I couldn't hang around once the
sheriff had been roused into action.'

Cartwright put a forkful of egg and ham into his

mouth, chewed, then spoke again. 'But he got excited when he heard the name Farraday?'

'Perhaps he's another Ranger. They often work in pairs.'

'But Harker told you he'd stolen his horse out in the scrubland. If he was also a Ranger that would be some coincidence.'

'Whether he is or not something has to be done about him.'

'I assume you mean something along the same lines that happened to Harker?'

Barclay nodded and lightly lifted the gun in his holster before allowing it to settle back.

For a few minutes silence reigned in the room, disturbed only by the sounds of Cartwright at work on his breakfast. Eventually, he spoke.

'Normally I wouldn't advocate violence, it has a nasty habit of attracting the attention of the law and the last thing we want is to come under scrutiny from any quarter. However, on this occasion it might strengthen our hand. Is he still in jail?'

'I don't know.'

'Find out and arrange his demise, preferably before the meeting at the courthouse. Make it a public event.'

Sol Barclay wasn't sure what was going on in Cartwright's mind but he was happy enough to comply with his plan. However, before he left the room, Cartwright had more instructions, which were not so pleasing to him.

'I don't want you involved.' Barclay looked quizzically at him. 'It's possible that people in the hotel here know of your association with me,' Cartwright told him, 'which wouldn't help my argument at the meeting.'

Barclay still didn't understand what Cartwright was planning to do but, none the less, he nodded his agreement.

'You know some people who can handle this?' asked Cartwright.

'It'll be done.' Sol Barclay quit the room with a confident grin.

Sammy Sutton was wearing a bright yellow shirt above tough blue riding pants when she entered the sheriff's office, but the colourful cheeriness of her apparel wasn't matched by the expression on her face. It was clear to Charlie Jefferson that a disagreement existed between her and Sheriff Agnew, who followed a step behind. No words were exchanged between them as she stood to one side of the door while the lawman crossed the room to the cells and, with the key he'd collected from his desk, unlocked Charlie's cell.

'You can go.'

Charlie followed him across the room to collect his holstered weapon, fastened it around his waist, then grabbed his hat from a peg near the door.

'What have you learned about the dead man?' he asked.

Sheriff Agnew hesitated, reluctant to answer because, clearly, his decision to detain Charlie had not found favour with Sammy Sutton nor, Charlie suspected, with her father.

'Nothing much,' he answered, 'apart from the fact that he turned up at the Rose of Texas last night where he ate a meal and rented a room. He was a stranger with little to say for himself. His saddlebags contained a change of clothes but there were no papers to say where he'd come from or why he was here. Nobody knows anything about him.'

'Somebody knows something, Sheriff, and they went to the trouble of finding him in your jail and putting a slug between his eyes. Perhaps if you find out where he was between stabling the Sutton horse and reaching the Rose of Texas you'll find the man called Farraday.'

'Still trying to tell me how to do my job,' Sheriff Agnew observed with obvious irritation.

Charlie ushered Sammy outside, it was clear by her expression that she had a question to ask.

'Farraday was the name that Harv Johnson spoke before dying. Is he connected with the killing in the jail, too?'

'Harker uttered the name just before he was shot. Whoever Farraday is and whatever his plans are he intends to pursue them ruthlessly.'

'What do you intend to do about it?' she asked.

'Me? It isn't my fight,' he replied. 'Only Harker could lead me to my saddle and rifle and with him dead I don't suppose I'll ever find them. I guess I'll ride out to your ranch, collect my horse and continue on my way.'

Passing through Charlie's mind was the fact that, without his saddle, he was unable to continue his journey. His red gelding was now Henry Sutton's property and even if he could garner enough money to buy the horse there would be nothing left over to buy supplies for the long journey to Wyoming. But even that wasn't the greatest impediment to the continuation of his journey home. Without the bonds that were sewn into the lining of his old saddle he would be unable to buy the land which he and Ruth Prescott had planned to make their home. He'd delayed his return home for three years in order to amass the wealth with which to realize their plans and now it was lost. Either he delayed his return until he had rebuilt his wealth or went home a half-starved saddle tramp.

Sammy was speaking, her voice reaching Charlie through his sombre thoughts. 'You're not leaving today?'

'Perhaps tomorrow,' he said without conviction.

The concern that had edged her voice with her question was replaced with a lighter note when she told him that this was a day of celebration in Mortimer, the anniversary of the founding of the town.

'There's a meeting in the courthouse at ten o'clock,' she told him, 'but after that the day is

62

given over to all kinds of competitions which take place along the riverbank. Tables are prepared with food and this evening there is a social get-together with music and dancing.'

'Sounds like fun,' said Charlie, although his tone seemed to be detached from the meaning of the words.

'Then you'll join us?' asked Sammy, smiling up into his face.'

Charlie shook his head. 'It's a party for citizens,' he said. 'Outsiders won't be welcome.'

'Nonsense,' she said. 'People come from miles around.'

'I don't know anyone in this town.'

Sammy put her hands on her hips, her expression matched the determination of her stance. 'You know me, and look,' she pointed down the street which Charlie now realized was festooned with banners and bunting, 'you know him.'

Charlie followed the line of her arm to a point twenty-five yards along the street where a slight figure could be seen sitting on the edge of a wooden water trough outside the mercantile building which, according to the wooden board affixed to the front of the building, was owned by George Gowland.

'Is that Dave Champion?' he asked.

'Yes. He came with Dad and me.'

Dave hadn't seen Sammy and Charlie, his attention being focused on covering the right holes of the pipe he was blowing into.

'Is he providing the music you spoke about?' asked Charlie.

Sammy regarded him with humour-filled admonishment. 'Perhaps next year. Come and say hello.'

Charlie shook his head and told the girl that an uncomfortable night in a prison cell had deprived him of any desire for celebration. In addition, he told her, he had no other clothes than those in which he'd been travelling, and he was in sore need of a bath and a shave.

'So right now I'm going to find a room.'

Sammy Sutton found it difficult to hide her disappointment. 'But you'll find us later?'

'Miss Sutton, you don't have to concern yourself about me. You must have friends a-plenty in this town. You and Dave should go and enjoy yourselves.'

'I wasn't just being polite or neighbourly,' she announced. 'I'd enjoy being with you.' She blushed slightly at her forwardness.

Charlie ran a hand over his jaw and studied her until her colouring grew deeper. 'And I'd enjoy being with you,' he said, 'but you don't know anything about me. Associating with me won't gain your father's approval.'

'My father won't object,' she argued.

'I can't take the risk,' Charlie said. 'He has my horse and at the moment I don't know how I'm going to buy him back.'

'You can have your horse,' she said. 'I'll speak to Father. It's rightly yours.'

'I appreciate your concern but your father would be out of pocket if I took it without payment, or he might make Eli Ringwood pay for it. Eli acted in good faith so it wouldn't be fair to punish him, would it? No, Miss Sutton, when it comes to horse trading there is a proper way to do things and deviation often brings bad repercussions.'

'Miss Sutton,' she said, angrily, with a slight quiver in her voice. 'Can't you call me Sammy, like everyone else?'

'No. I'll never call you Sammy. You are a young woman who deserves to be addressed correctly. Go along now, perhaps we'll meet later, if not then I hope to see you when I come to collect the red.'

Sammy Sutton thought she was being dismissed like a child and she was wounded by that belief. Without a word, mainly because she suspected that her disappointment would become too obvious to Charlie, she turned her back and headed down the street to join Dave Champion.

Sheriff Agnew, who had quit his office a few steps behind Charlie and the girl, stopped shoulder to shoulder with Charlie.

'Remember what I told you,' he said. 'I don't want you hanging around town any longer than is necessary.'

'That might be some time,' replied Charlie. 'I was robbed and the man who did it was killed in your jail.'

Sheriff Agnew was unimpressed. 'Ride out before nightfall,' he told Charlie.

'That's part of the problem, Sheriff. I no longer have a horse, nor the money to buy another.'

'Harker's pockets weren't full of money and no one's reported that he was spending heavily before I arrested him last night.'

'He didn't know the value of what he'd stolen from me.' Charlie's words carried little volume, nothing more than a thought escaping through his mouth.

'Tonight,' Sheriff Agnew said, instilling into the word a note of finality as he began to move away.

Charlie knew it had been his own brusque behaviour when he'd arrived in Mortimer that had generated the sheriff's main gripe against him. No one, especially lawmen, likes to be criticized for the way he goes about his business, and Charlie had implied that Abe Agnew was failing in his duty by refusing to ride out to the Sutton ranch immediately to investigate the death of Harv Johnson.

'We got off on the wrong foot, Sheriff,' Charlie said. 'I'm not responsible for any of yesterday's troubles. I was riding north, heading for my home in Wyoming. Until recently I was working for the government in Arkansas and Kansas. If you contact Captain Jessop at Fort Smith, Arkansas, he'll vouch for me.'

'Have you been soldiering?'

'Not since the war, but lately I've been working

with the army.' Charlie didn't want to go into details. It wasn't everyone who approved of the fight against the bands of Rebels who had continued raiding after the surrender of the Confederate army at Appomattox, especially in a Southern state like Texas.

'Captain Jessop,' mused Sheriff Agnew, a glint in his eye betraying the fact that he probably knew the role Charlie had been playing in the states further east. 'Perhaps I will check you out,' he said; then he turned on his heel and headed along the street towards the courthouse.

For a brief moment, Charlie watched as the lawman walked the street, touching his hat in greeting as he passed townsfolk along the way. Charlie rubbed his jaw, remembered the bath, shave and sleep he'd promised himself and stepped off the boardwalk on to the hard, dusty street. That step down saved his life.

Without warning, a bullet smacked into the wooden balcony support in front of which he'd been standing and a cascade of splinters flew into the air. The report from the firing of the weapon carried across the street and, as he threw himself to the ground, Charlie saw a wisp of smoke rising from a gap between the buildings which were the places of business for a barber and a milliner. Charlie dragged his pistol from its holster and, at sight of a figure behind the slim line of smoke, pulled the trigger. There was a click as the hammer fell on an empty chamber.

Once more Charlie pulled the trigger and got the same result. It passed through his mind that the shells must have been removed when he'd been arrested, and now he was facing a gunman with an empty weapon. People who had been moving lazily on the boardwalk were now scattering for cover, while across the street, encouraged by the metallic clicks, the gunman stepped forward, certain that Charlie Jefferson was at his mercy.

From his left, a shout carried to Charlie, but not until his assailant turned his head to investigate did Charlie cast a look in that direction. Sheriff Agnew was hurrying along the street, pistol drawn, ordering a ceasefire. While the gunman was distracted, Charlie took the opportunity to seek protection behind a couple of crates on the boardwalk behind him.

A pistol was fired, a bullet spanged off at an angle after striking a metal clasp on the crate. A second shot was fired but this time no bullet came in Charlie's direction. The sheriff, he supposed, had discharged his weapon to enforce his authority. Gingerly, Charlie raised his head, hopeful that the sheriff now had the situation under control. Those hopes were dashed. Sheriff Abe Agnew lay face down in the street, spread-eagled, and the big pistol that a few moments earlier had been wielded with authority by the lawman now lay uselessly in the dirt, inches from his outstretched fingers.

In the hubbub, voices were raised, hurried foot-falls sounded on the planks, horses neighed and a dog barked. Another shot was fired but the gunman had taken careless aim, reacting too quickly to the sight of Charlie's raised head. When, once more, Charlie dipped his head behind the crate it was with the knowledge that a second gunman had killed the sheriff and he now had little chance of escape. He'd had only a swift view of both men but it had been enough to convince him that he didn't know either of them. It seemed likely that he would die without ever learning the cause of their grudge against him.

Making a dash for the sheriff's discarded weapon seemed to be his only chance, but he knew that the moment he broke from cover the two men would have him in a cross-fire. Still, he counselled himself, it was better to go down fighting than to be caught on his knees and be put to death like a rabid dog.

The low murmur of bystanders reached his ears but no one, it seemed, was prepared to step forward to help him. It was a private fight, no doubt they would learn the cause of it when the gun smoke had cleared. He heard a woman's voice, shrill with horror-filled emotion, announcing to everyone along the length of the street that the sheriff had been murdered. Drumming hoof beats sounded, a horse was running along the street, getting closer, and the murmurs of the citizens carried a different message, one of surprise and expectation.

Again, a gunshot cracked in the street and there

were shouts of dismay from the watchers. Charlie risked another look. A brown-and-white piebald was rearing in the middle of the street, spooked, Charlie presumed, by the gunshot. Its rider had been unseated and was about to hit the ground heavily, close to Charlie. The still stomping horse was performing circles as though it had been circus-trained, and by good chance it was preventing the gunmen from getting a clear shot at either Charlie or the tumbling rider.

The figure in the yellow shirt and blue pants hit the ground with a grunt, and though Charlie could barely believe that Sammy Sutton had risked her life to reach him his reaction was instant. Jumping on to the street he drew a wild shot from his first assailant but, careless now of his own safety, he rolled along the ground in an effort to cover the girl with his own body. But Sammy Sutton had another surprise for Charlie Jefferson. In her right hand she held the barrel of a long saddle-gun.

Charlie Jefferson had been in dangerous situations in the past and the desire to preserve his life had produced moments of quick thinking and instant reaction that were instinctive rather than intelligent, but now, with the life of the brave young girl also in his hands he seized the rifle, thrust himself forward under the belly of the piebald and fired two shots with deadly accuracy. Both men were lifted from their feet as a heavy bullet struck each heart.

For some moments, while the gun smoke drifted away and the horse settled, the street was silent, but by the time Charlie had raised the girl from the ground some townspeople were gathering around the pair while others were talking over the three bodies in the street.

Sammy Sutton sagged against Charlie, not only because of the pain in her shoulder where she'd hit the ground, but also because the realization that death had been close at hand was sucking away her strength. Charlie could feel her trembling against his chest. His instinct was to tell her she was a fool for taking such a risk but he didn't: to have done so would have undervalued her bravery that deserved praise not chastisement. She had saved his life, of that there was no doubt.

When Henry Sutton arrived, breathless and his face grey with the knowledge of how close he had been to losing his daughter, he had no hesitation in pointing out how foolhardy her action had been.

'Come with me,' he told her. 'I'll get you a room at the hotel. You can rest there while I go to the meeting at the courthouse.' With a look of anger for Charlie he led his daughter down the street to the Hotel of the Republic.

71

CHAPTER SEVEN

The courthouse doors were still closed to the general public but inside half a dozen men had assembled to finalize the strategy for the meeting ahead. Four of the company were the most influential men in Mortimer. Dustin Baker, the mayor, occupied the most central seat at the long table that had been placed on a raised dais. To his right were the Templeton brothers, Curt and Joel who, between them, owned most of the grazing land north of Mortimer and were landlords to most of the tradesmen in the town. To the left of the mayor the banker, Oliver Calloway, fidgeted with some papers. He was trying to maintain an outward calm that was at loggerheads with his inner turmoil and the uncertainty that had kept sleep at bay for the past two nights. As the primary source of financial knowledge and advice in Mortimer he had taken on the role of town treasurer in addition to his duties at the bank. The success of the venture that was about to be presented to the citizens would, he believed, not only elevate the low level of respect he currently enjoyed in the town, but would also get him noticed by head office, which would, he prayed, produce a long-wanted return East and the offer of one of the most highly paid managerial posts.

The other two men in the room were Thomas Cartwright and Sol Barclay, the latter lounging at the back of the room and taking no part in the discussion that was under way.

'I received a message last night,' Cartwright told the representatives of the town council, 'and it isn't good news.' Four pairs of eyes were fixed on him, waiting for more information. 'Somehow, details of the proposed Transcontinental Railroad route have reached the ears of the committee of a town called Gatling which is almost three hundred miles north of here, and they, being astute men like yourselves, have also realized the value of a spur line for their social and economic development and are proposing to submit an application to the railroad.'

'Why is that bad news for us?' asked Curt Templeton.

'Because the Transcontinental is already operating on a stretched budget and they can't afford to build a spur line to every settlement between here and California.'

'But you've submitted our proposal, haven't you? Why would Gatling's offer take precedence over ours?'

73

Cartwright didn't hurry with his reply, shuffled his feet as though his audience might be embarrassed by what he had to say.

'Gatling's a bigger town that suffered little during the war. In short, it's wealthier than Mortimer and perhaps they'll be prepared to put up more than the fifty per cent that you are offering. In addition, it is closer to the main line which will mean that resources are diverted for a shorter period.'

The townsmen exchanged looks but it was the mayor who put their obvious question into words.

'Are you telling us that the railroad won't come to Mortimer? That our plans for the development of the town are scuppered?'

'Not necessarily,' Cartwright replied, 'but the only chance requires swift action.'

'What do you mean?' asked Curt Templeton.

'I mean the railroad won't refuse hard cash. I know we'd planned to raise the first instalment over the next two months, but if I can get a portion of your money to them before the Gatling proposition is lodged then they'll be obliged to honour the agreement.'

'Do you think that would work?' Mayor Baker looked to his fellow councillors for comments.

The conversation had reached the point where Oliver Calloway, the banker, was in his element.

'How much do you think it will take to close the deal?' he asked.

Cartwright spread his arms, a gesture that

implied he couldn't give an accurate answer.

'My advice would be to gather in as much as you have available in the bank and in your personal strongboxes. Mr Barclay and I will leave on tonight's stage and we should have the money with the railroad in five days.'

The four leading citizens of Mortimer formed a huddle and while they murmured Cartwright crossed the room to join Sol Barclay. At that moment the unmistakeable crack of a pistol shot reached them from the street. Following more gunshots and at Cartwright's behest, Sol Barclay quit the courtroom to discover the cause of the shooting, although both men believed they already knew the identity of the victim.

When he returned it was with the news that the sheriff was dead. He caught Cartwright's eye and with a slight shake of his head conveyed the news that the plot to kill Charlie Jefferson had failed. While the mayor and his colleagues considered the dreadful news, Cartwright pulled Barclay to one side and was informed that the men who had been hired for the task were lying in the street with the sheriff. Cartwright's anger only showed in his eyes.

'After the meeting I'll remain in the hotel,' he said. 'If all goes well we'll be on the stage out of here before nightfall.'

Their conversation was cut short as townsfolk arrived for the start of the meeting.

*

Mayor Baker began proceedings with a short address that outlined the council's vision for the future of the town. If it was to thrive, he told the assembly, then it must be prepared to embrace the changes that would surely follow as Texas strived for reconstruction after the defeat of the Confederacy.

'It is our desire,' he informed his audience in stentorian tones, 'to promote Mortimer so that it becomes a major player in this state in the years ahead. To that end, we,' and at that point he spread his arms to include the Templeton brothers and Oliver Calloway, 'have held discussions with Mr Cartwright,' this time he indicated the man on his left who was a stranger to everyone else in the room, 'a representative of the railroad company who intend to lay tracks about a hundred miles north of here.'

There were murmurs of interest among those gathered although no one could fathom why the building of a railroad so far to the north could affect their town.

'Through the good offices of Mr Cartwright,' he continued, 'we have an opportunity to establish a spur line to Mortimer. Not only will that give us the speediest possible access to all points east and west, but it will attract new people and new business, which will establish our town as one of the most modern and forward-thinking in the entire state.'

The chatter among the audience grew louder. Mayor Baker raised his arms in an appeal for silence.

'Of course,' following the tone of achievement in which his words had so far been uttered he now adopted a deeper, more serious note, 'there is a cost to be paid up front before the future benefits can be achieved.'

'A cost?' someone called. 'You mean we have to pay them to come here?'

'We'll have to pay a portion of the costs. The railroad has limited resources; finance has to be raised for every portion of track and, of course, building a spur line can cause a delay to the main project. Time is money, friends, and the railroad is being built to a tight schedule. Theirs is a continental enterprise on to which we are hoping to attach ourselves. The profit in terms of the town's growth and stature will be, ultimately, worth the investment.'

'How much will the investment be?' The speaker was John Stewart who produced the weekly newspaper.

'Fifty per cent.'

Mayor Baker's reply was spoken as though the amount was no more than the cost of two shots of whiskey at the Rose of Texas, but it brought gasps of astonishment from some of the men in the room. When John Stewart spoke his words reflected the view of the assembly.

'That's a lot of money.'

'We don't have to find it all immediately,' the mayor replied, which elicited a few laughs, none of which were laced with humour. 'A figure of two hundred thousand dollars has been agreed in the first instance, the rest to be paid either in cash, goods or services as the work progresses. It's a good deal.'

Henry Sutton, who had been one of the last to arrive following the attention he'd needed to give to his daughter's welfare, pushed his way forward.

'And how do you hope to raise two hundred thousand dollars?'

'The town has money that has been levied in taxes. With the permission of this meeting we will use some of that and raise the rest by individual subscription. To convince you of the worthiness of this enterprise both Mr Curt Templeton and Mr Joel Templeton are prepared to make a large donation to the cause, as am I, and Mr Calloway is actively seeking the support of the bank.'

Dropping names had the desired effect; those seated at the table could see heads nodding in conversation with their neighbours and although there was no outcry of support the mood was definitely in favour of the proposal. Only Henry Sutton seemed doubtful and when the mayor added that he was seeking donations from other landowners and businessmen, Henry asked what benefit there was for him.

'It's all well and good being public spirited,' he said, 'but you're asking for money that I've earned and I don't see that there is any profit in it. I don't intend to go travelling either east or west; there's enough work on my spread to keep me busy until the angel's trumpet sounds.'

A few people laughed, one or two were interested to hear Mayor Baker's reply but it was Curt Templeton who spoke.

'Henry, you're running a huge herd these days and it takes you and a handful of men several weeks to get your cattle to market. If, instead, you were able to load them on to a train here in Mortimer you'd save all that time away from the ranch, save yourself the overhead of extra crew for the drive and you'd be able to send them to the best-paying markets in the country. Joel and I have studied on this, Henry, and we're fully in favour of the scheme.'

Henry Sutton knew the Templeton brothers to be careful and successful businessmen, so he acknowledged that if they approved it was probably a good idea.

Mayor Baker was talking again, telling them of the threat from Gatling and the need to act quickly. His words were backed up by Thomas Cartwright, who spoke to the meeting for the first time.

'I've only been in your town a short while,' he began, speaking slowly and clearly like a practised orator, 'and I like what I see. I agree with your mayor and your prominent citizens: this is a good town with a vitality that deserves to be rewarded. Put the bad days of the war behind you and look to the future. As Mayor Baker has told you, you are now in a race with another town to win the only spur line that will be laid in this part of Texas and you must act with all urgency. I say that not just because of the competition from Gatling, but because of the events of this morning. I'm talking about the slaughter on your main street and the death of your appointed law officer.

'I know that there are good people in this town; however the decision-makers of the railroad will not take that into account. If news reaches them that this is a violent, lawless community they will be reluctant to lay their lines here. So I urge you, if you want your town to be a vibrant part of the new Texas, then act immediately. In the next few hours gather up every cent that can be spared and I'll set out on the evening coach. In five days I'll put it in the hands of the railroad treasurer, thereby ensuring a great future for Mortimer.'

A few men cheered at the end of Cartwright's speech and there was a great deal of grinning and back-slapping, as though each of them had just inherited a gold mine. Mayor Baker announced himself available to receive individual subscriptions, adding that each donation would be recorded and repaid when the town had sufficient funds to reimburse the donors, whose names would be inscribed on a roll of honour to ensure that they were remembered by future generations.

A show of hands was all that was necessary for the mayor's proposal to be accepted and soon the process of collecting donations began. Thomas Cartwright returned to the seclusion of his hotel room where he intended to wait until the collection was delivered to him. A target amount had been abandoned; he was content to take as much as the town could raise within the next few hours. Quitting Mortimer was now imperative, not only before his status as a representative of the Transcontinental Railroad Company came under greater scrutiny, but also before he was identified as Courtney Farraday, wanted by the Texas Rangers as the perpetrator of a similar swindle near the Louisiana border some months earlier.

As he and Sol Barclay took the back route from the courthouse to the hotel he issued orders that would help them to elude pursuit once they were clear of the town.

CHAPTER EIGHT

When Henry Sutton had acquired a room for his daughter at the Hotel of the Republic he'd chased away Dave Champion so that Sammy could rest and compose herself. The young lad had wandered around hoping to fall in with some people of his own age but, as most people were heading for the courthouse, the main street had become a quiet and lonely place. Then he saw Charlie Jefferson standing on the veranda outside the Rose of Texas and ran across to join him.

'Gee, Mr Jefferson,' he began, 'that was some shooting. Who were those men?' Before Charlie could answer that question Dave posed another. 'Were you surprised when Sammy rode between you and those gunmen?'

Charlie nodded; yes, he had been surprised but he still wasn't clear in his mind whether he was angry with the girl for such reckless behaviour or just grateful that her unexpected intervention had

saved his life. The latter, of course, was true regardless of the former, he was conscious of the fact that
it had been an act of outstanding bravery, but could-
n't understand why she had done it; they barely
knew each other, had exchanged nothing more
than a handful of words.

Dave was talking, explaining how Sammy had
tried to persuade other bystanders to intervene
when it had become clear that there were no shells
in Charlie's gun. Then, when the sheriff got shot,
without another word she'd leapt into her saddle
and galloped up the street.

'We thought she'd been hit when her horse
reared and she fell to the ground,' Dave confided,
'but it turned out to be a ploy to get her rifle to
you.'

'She was very brave,' said Charlie.

Dave seemed to take Charlie's words as a criticism. 'I suppose I should have been the one to
intervene,' he said. 'It was wrong to leave it to a
girl.'

Charlie rubbed Dave's hair. 'No. It wasn't your
fight and, grateful as I am for what she did, I'm just
pleased that Miss Sutton came to no worse harm
than a bruising from the fall.'

They walked in silence for a few minutes. Charlie
said he was looking for a barber shop but every-
where seemed to be closed for business.

'Everyone's at the town meeting, I suppose,' Dave
informed him, 'but Mr Clarke's shop is on the next

block. He should be back shortly. He has a bath-house out back, too.'

Promising himself a later visit to Mr Clarke's shop, Charlie walked with Dave down to the stretch of ground along the riverbank where the events were scheduled to take place. Dave wanted to know if Charlie was going to enter any of the competitions or races, and when Charlie realized that there were money prizes to be won he was tempted, but a fee was required to enter and he couldn't risk any of the small amount of money that remained in his pocket.

By the time they'd navigated the fête area and discovered that there were to be foot races, horse races, prizefighting, rifle shooting, pie and cake stalls and a dozen other events, Charlie's stomach was grumbling. Little food had come his way since the plate of stew he'd been served at the stage station the previous day. When he and Dave returned to the main street the groups of men dotted here and there along the boardwalks bore testimony to the fact that the meeting at the courthouse had concluded. One or two heads turned in Charlie's direction as he passed and he knew that those who had witnessed the earlier incident on the street were pointing him out to those who had not. He thought he recognized a couple of cowboys from the Sutton place, especially one wearing a red shirt and a long moustache who, yesterday, had kicked at a rock in the ground as though uninterested in Charlie's plea for information. Now he leant against a rail and tipped his hat forward to cover his eyes while his companions openly watched Charlie's progress towards the barber's shop.

Zeke Clarke, like every other barber whose chair Charlie had sat in, never stopped talking. He'd ask a question but would seldom wait for an answer, streaming out words that might or might not have relevance to his chosen topic.

'Are you just here for the celebration? I've been here seven years now. It's a good town, thriving, and a railroad link would be a great thing. Yessir, I can see the advantage. What about you, are you in favour? Of course, generating money to pay for it isn't going to be easy. Dustin Baker may have dreams and plans for Mortimer but I didn't hear how it's going to be paid for other than by public contribution. I may be busy but I don't make a lot of profit from a fifty-cent haircut.'

Charlie didn't know what the barber was talking about but it didn't seem as though an opinion was required. So, between Zeke Clarke's chatter, the increasingly wearisome sound of Dave Champion's pipe and the general fatigue by which Charlie was beset, he was almost asleep as Zeke's razor scraped over his jaw.

'Are you Charlie Jefferson?'

The voice was loud, but strangely it carried no hint of threat. Still, it startled both the barber and his customer. Zeke Clarke, turning to identify the man in the doorway deftly lifted his razor away from

Charlie's throat, while Charlie's eyes opened but he had to wait a few moments until the man had shuffled his way into a position where his face could be seen in the mirror.

He was a big man, more than six feet high and wide and round, like an overgrown child with puppy fat that had never been shed. He was wearing grubby canvas trousers, a grey shirt and a once-white, wide-brimmed Stetson with a high crown. A badge was pinned to his shirt pocket. In his left hand he held a slip of paper.

'Charlie Jefferson?' he enquired again.

'That's me,' said Charlie.

'I'm Horry Blackstone. I'm Sheriff Agnew's deputy. That is, I was his deputy. Part-time deputy, he called on me when he needed help.'

Charlie guessed that Sheriff Agnew hadn't called on him often or for anything important.

'What can I do for you?' he asked.

Horry Blackstone shuffled his feet and tried to put some authority into his voice when he spoke.

'You can tell me what all that shooting was about earlier and why Sheriff Agnew got killed.'

'I would help you if I could, Deputy, but I didn't know the men who attacked me.'

'You didn't know them?' Horry found Charlie's statement difficult to believe.

'No.'

'Nor why they attacked you?'

'It could be because of a man called Farraday. His

86

name was on the lips of a dying man out on the Sutton range and it was the name uttered by the prisoner who was killed in the jailhouse last night. Do you know anyone called Farraday?'

At that moment, the room seemed to darken, as though someone else had taken up a position in the doorway thereby preventing the sun from doing its job, but the doorway wasn't directly behind Charlie, it was at an angle beyond the scope of the mirror. Charlie assumed that it was another customer but for the moment he was more interested in hearing Horry Blackstone's answer.

It was no surprise to learn that the deputy didn't know anyone in Mortimer by the name of Farraday, Charlie had thought it unlikely that the gauche fellow would know more people than the sheriff. Charlie turned his attention to the barber but he, too, shook his head. If Farraday was in Mortimer, Charlie decided, he wasn't making any impression on its citizens. When he got the chance he turned his head to ask the newcomer if he was familiar with the name, but there was no one else in the room. Horry raised the piece of paper he was carrying.

'This telegraph message came for the sheriff from Fort Smith. It says you were employed by the military as a special agent.'

'That's not information you should be announcing in a public place,' Charlie told him. 'You're the head lawman in Mortimer now; you'll have to learn to keep secrets.'

Those words flustered Horry. It was clear from his expression that he doubted his ability to carry out the most menial of duties; being head lawman was way beyond his capabilities.

'I wondered why the sheriff was checking up on you,' he said, guilelessly.

'Perhaps he checked up on everyone who came to town so that he could keep an eye on trouble-makers.'

Horry Blackmore considered Charlie's explanation and accepted it. 'I don't suppose he would have kept you in jail if he'd got this information last night.'

'Perhaps not,' said Charlie. 'I hope that means that you're not going to put me back there because of the killings this morning.'

'Why would I do that?' asked Horry. 'You killed the men who killed the sheriff.'

Zeke Clarke cleared the remaining foam from Charlie's face and pointed the way to the bath-house. As Charlie reached in his pocket for some coins he glanced out of the window to where Dave Champion still waited, but the lad was no longer playing his pipe because he had company. The cowboy with the moustache, the one Charlie thought he'd seen at the Sutton ranch, was talking to Dave. It didn't seem unlikely that they would know each other, they might even have travelled from the Sutton ranch together that morning.

Suddenly, the cowboy flipped a small coin in a high loop towards Dave; then, without a backward glance, set off across the street towards one of the now busy saloons.

Half an hour later, having almost fallen asleep in the warm water and afterwards having tarred the dust out of the only clothes he possessed, Charlie stepped on to the street almost refreshed, almost tidy, certainly hungry. Dave Champion stopped piping so that he could greet him.

'I've got a message for you, Mr Jefferson.'

Charlie was surprised to find himself hoping the answer would be Samantha Sutton when he asked who it was from.

'I don't know his name. A man gave me a dime to tell you he had the information you wanted.'

Charlie recalled the cowboy with the moustache flipping a coin to Dave and, when asked, Dave confirmed that he was the one who had sent the message, but he didn't think he worked for Henry Sutton. 'He's a stranger in town.'

'Are you sure the message is for me?' asked Charlie.

'Of course. He asked your name, said he'd seen us together earlier.'

Charlie knew that that was true, although the man had feigned unconcern, he hadn't fooled Charlie.

'What's the message?'

'He wants to meet you at the livery stable. He said

to wait until the horse races had begun along the riverside.'

Charlie wondered if the cowboy was the man called Farraday and if he would be walking into a trap if he went to Gus Brewer's stable. After paying Dave, Charlie had seen the man cross the street to the Double Diamond. Perhaps he was still there and perhaps it would be to Charlie's advantage to take the initiative. He slid his pistol out of its holster, checked that each chamber was loaded, then left the boardwalk and took the first pace across the street.

'Here's Sammy,' Dave said, and Charlie stopped to watch the approaching girl.

The eager, jaunty manner of her walk and the smile on her face dismissed any need for enquiries as to her well-being; it was clear that Samantha Sutton had fully recovered from both the physical and mental aspects of the earlier incident, and because of the brightness of her appearance, Charlie was glad that he'd washed away the dust of recent days. He removed his hat while he talked to her, expressing his gratitude for her intervention and speaking of her bravery. Remembering the expression on her father's face when he'd taken her to the hotel, Charlie figured there was no need to dwell on the foolishness of her behaviour, or to stress the danger into which she had put herself, Henry Sutton would have had much to say on those topics. So, unwillingly, he disappointed her when she announced her hope that he would go to the riverside events with her and Dave Champion.

Charlie's excuse was his hunger and the fact that he couldn't afford to eat anywhere better than the Rose of Texas or one of the other saloons, which were unsuitable venues for the daughter of Henry Sutton. Indeed, Charlie suggested that her father would disapprove of any association between his daughter and himself because he was little more than a stranger to the territory. Bearing in mind the earlier event, they would be supplying the town gossips with plenty of ammunition if they were seen walking together in familiar fashion.

Of course, for himself, Charlie cared little for the tittle-tattle of the townswomen or for the disapproval of Henry Sutton, but Samantha's reputation mattered because she had to live in the town after he moved on. In truth, he recognized the fact that his liking for the girl was greater than it ought to be for a man returning home to marry his pre-war sweetheart. Samantha was pretty, her face and figure pleased him, but more important to him was her desire to help people. That was how they'd met: her going to the assistance of a shot man and taking control of the situation when Charlie had joined her. She was young yet resourceful and there could be no better demonstration of that than her intervention earlier in the day when he'd been at the mercy of a gunman.

So it wasn't easy to snub her invitation, or to see

the hurt that the rejection etched upon her face, but he couldn't encourage the girl's interest in him, nor could he keep her at his side when the message he'd received from the cowboy with the moustache could be an invitation to an ambush. He couldn't place her or young Dave Champion in danger. Instead, he replaced his hat, wished them a fun-filled afternoon and took another step across the street towards the Double Diamond. But once again he was stopped in his tracks after only one stride.

Three men were bustling down the street towards him. In the lead was a man in store-bought clothes with a brown derby on his head. He wasn't tall and had the girth of a man who was a stranger to manual work. At his side strode a taller man who, although slicked-up in smart clothes, had the stride of a man who had spent a long time in the saddle. He had a sharp expression in his eyes which bright-ened the weather-hammered wrinkled face. Behind those two was a lumbering figure whom Charlie rec-ognized: Horry Blackmore. They stopped in front of Charlie.

'Sammy,' said the first man as he doffed his derby hat in greeting, 'you're looking as pretty as a picture on this lovely day. Mr Jefferson,' he continued, his words coming quickly to prevent interruption, 'my name is Dustin Baker and I'm the mayor of Mortimer.' He thrust out his hand for Charlie to shake. 'This is Curt Templeton,' he added as he inclined his head to the man on his left, 'and I believe you've already met Deputy Blackmore.'

Charlie acknowledged the other two men.

'Abe Agnew had been sheriff here in Mortimer for many years,' stated the mayor. 'He grew with the town, not just a good lawman but a dedicated citizen who will be sorely missed.'

'Amen to that,' said Curt Templeton as though he'd been waiting for an opportunity to speak.

'His unexpected death,' continued Dustin Baker, 'leaves the town vulnerable. We believe that you can help us.'

'I'm at a loss to know how,' Charlie told him.

A conspiratorial smile touched the mayor's face. 'It is our understanding that you have some experience of law enforcement and that a telegraph message intended for Abe endorsed your capabilities.'

Charlie looked towards Horry Blackmore and the deputy hastily looked at the ground to avoid the accusatory glance. At the same moment, Charlie sensed that the statement had caught the attention of Samantha and Dave, both of whom stepped closer to listen to the conversation.

Mayor Baker was still speaking. 'We want you to be our sheriff. Much as the members of the town committee appreciate the efforts of the remaining deputies, none of them has the necessary experience to be sheriff.'

'Neither do I,' Charlie told him. 'It's true that for a while I was a government agent, but I'm afraid you've misunderstood my role. I was working with the army, not policing a town.'

The mayor wasn't to be put off. 'It doesn't have to be a permanent appointment,' he bargained. 'Just a few weeks until we can organize a replacement. We're a town with ambitions, Mr Jefferson, and those ambitions could suffer a serious set-back if we lose a grip on the order imposed by Abe Agnew. When respect for the law slips a town can quickly descend into chaos. We can't afford to let that happen.'

'I'm sorry gentlemen. I'll be heading north as soon as I can get together enough money to buy back my horse.'

'We'll give you a horse. A good horse, the best in town, the horse of your choice and we'll pay you a fee on top of that.'

Charlie didn't doubt his ability to do the job and he was tempted by the prospect of coins in his pocket and a horse under him. In addition, despite her efforts to hide her true feelings, Samantha Sutton's wide-eyed expression betrayed her eagerness for him to accept a job that would keep him longer in Mortimer and it was an expression he couldn't ignore.

'Thanks for the offer,' he told the town committee men, 'but it's not for me.' He touched his hat and this time he completed his walk to the doors of the Double Diamond.

From the boardwalk, and before pushing

through the batwing doors, Charlie scanned the interior of the saloon, seeking out the moustachioed cowboy in the red shirt, but without success. Either he had slipped out while Charlie had been engaged in conversation or he occupied one of the upstairs rooms. Charlie took a table which gave him a view of the staircase and the street door, ordered a meal and settled down to wait for the cowboy's return or until it was time to keep his appointment at the livery stable.

CHAPTER NINE

In his room in the Hotel of the Republic Thomas Cartwright sloshed whiskey into a tumbler from a near-empty bottle, then wandered over to the window to look down on the quiet street.

'This would be a good time for you to leave,' he told Sol Barclay. 'Everyone's quit town, gone down to the celebrations along the riverbank.' He took a sip from the glass, then chuckled. 'Sort of completes a circle, doesn't it? On the anniversary of the founding of the town they've bankrupted it.' He glanced at his companion and it was clear that Barclay saw no humour in the situation. Cartwright wondered if the man in the black clothes was ever amused by anything.

'Now,' he added, 'you know what to do.'

Barclay said he did but it was clear that Cartwright wanted him to repeat the plan so, with ill-grace, he did so. 'I'll wait somewhere close to the relay station where the horses can have a good rest.'

'You're sure that there is an overnight stop?'

'Certain. Normally they go through to the next relay station, but as the departure has been delayed because of the celebration it would be dark before they got halfway there.'

'OK.'

'When all the lights are out I'll come down to collect you.'

'We'll be clear of this territory before the sun rises and no one will know in which direction we've fled.' He laughed at the simplicity of the scheme, could barely believe that people were so gullible, especially those who gained positions of authority. Blinded by their own importance they were willing to grasp at any scheme that seemed to fulfil their ambition. 'You just have to find the right fool,' he muttered to himself.

Sol Barclay moved towards the door but Cartwright stopped him, grabbed a soft bag from the corner of the room and gave it to his accomplice.

'A change of clothes,' he told him, 'I can't go riding through rough country in these garments.'

'What about the money?' asked Barclay. 'When do we share it out?'

'You'll get what you're due tomorrow when we're well clear of the relay station. Then we'll split trails, too. You and I won't meet again.'

'This extra work I've done, taking care of the

Ranger and Harker in jail, they deserve an extra payment.'

'Sure, sure,' agreed Cartwright, 'but until I find out how much money the good townspeople believe will buy them a branch line, I don't know how much it will be.' He raised his glass to toast the future. 'Until tomorrow, Mr Barclay, when we'll both be wealthy men.'

Barclay took the bag from Cartwright and quit the room, leaving Cartwright to muse over how small an amount he would need to pay to be rid of the gunman.

Barclay, too, wondered what trivial amount Cartwright would offer and whether, when they reached the parting of the ways, he would have to kill the dandified man. With these thoughts in his mind he slipped out of the back door of the hotel and worked his way through the narrow alleyways to Gus Brewer's stable.

Although he was unlikely to be interrupted, Sol chose not to open wide the high doors in order to flood the interior with sunlight. Instead, in the semi-gloom, he worked his way along the stalls, found the horses he wanted, then loaded each with saddle, bridle and blanket collected from the tack rail. He had just tightened the final buckle when he heard approaching footsteps. Reluctant to be seen, he crouched down in the corner of the stall and waited for the newcomer to conduct his own business and then leave. Barclay hoped the man would be quick because he wanted to be clear of the stable before people began returning to town from the events at the riverside.

But the man showed no signs of urgency. Once inside, he pushed the high doors closer together, thereby diminishing the amount of light that entered the stable. Then he moved to the back of the building, failing to see that two of the stalled horses had been harnessed for travel, or even to suspect that anyone else loitered within the building. Nothing about the shuffling and snorting of one or two of the beasts signified anything out of the ordinary to him as he made his way along the central aisle.

Sol Barclay figured that the newcomer was waiting for someone, so he too would have to wait. It became a wait of several minutes and Barclay knew that he was trapped there until the other man departed.

Meanwhile, when the barman stated that he, too, would like to join in with the celebrations that were being enjoyed by the rest of the citizens of Mortimer, Charlie Jefferson, being the last customer in the Double Diamond, took the hint and stepped outside. Apart from the patient horses that were hitched at every pole along its length, the main street was deserted. Every door was closed; all business, it seemed, had been concluded for the day. Charlie paused on the boardwalk, keeping close to the wall of the building where the shadows were deepest so that he was less of a target if the message had been sent to lure him into a trap.

From the direction of the river the sound of a cheering crowd, rising in a crescendo, announced that a race was reaching a thrilling climax. Charlie turned his head in that direction. Involuntarily his thoughts strayed to Samantha Sutton who, with young Dave Champion, would be among those spectators. With annoyance he remembered the disappointment that had shown on her face when he rejected Mayor Baker's offer. Although he knew he had done the right thing for the right reason it still rankled that it had been necessary to inflict pain on the girl who had risked everything to save his life. Perhaps sometime in the future there would be an opportunity to repay her, but for now he had an appointment to keep and he began to move away from the noise of the crowd to the far end of the street where Gus Brewer's livery stable was situated.

Charlie had had little opportunity to familiarize himself with the layout of the town but he recalled that there were corrals behind the big stable building which had a small door at the back to give the stableman access to the livestock. He knew that if he was walking into an ambush it was probable that that door would be no less under observation than those at the front, but at least by taking advantage of the narrow alleys behind the main street his approach would not be under constant observation.

100

So that was what he did, cutting down the side of the bank and taking a long detour around the Hotel of the Republic, then ducking under the bars of the corral and manoeuvring a route through the gathered horses before making a final dash to the back of the stable.

With gun in hand he opened the door slowly and was greeted by the usual smells of manure and leather. It was dark inside even though the high, far doors were partly open, permitting a narrow shaft of daylight in which straw motes hovered, raised by the handful of curious horses in the stalls. Charlie slipped inside and pressed himself into the darkness at the back of the stable. For several moments he remained motionless, giving his eyes the chance to become accustomed to the dim light and hoping that anyone already inside would betray their presence.

He advanced two steps; then a voice, low and heavy with a Southern accent, came from Charlie's right.

'Put away the gun, Mr Jefferson, I've got you covered.'

For a moment, Charlie considered an act of resistance; if he threw himself to the ground he could perhaps in the interior gloom roll into one of the stalls and from there engage his foe. However, his mind was processing facts quickly and it was clear to him that such a course of action had little hope of success. He had no idea how long his opponent had been waiting, but his eyes had become sufficiently accustomed to the reduced light to know Charlie's location and that he had his gun unholstered. It was also apparent from his voice that the man was very close and therefore unlikely to miss his target if Charlie made a wrong move. Most important, unlike the two men who had attacked him earlier in the day, this man hadn't opened fire at the first opportunity, which suggested that he didn't mean to kill him here in the stable.

Charlie slid his gun into its holster and waited. A man emerged from the nearest stall, his appearance, with the light behind him, nothing more than a silhouette, yet Charlie recognized the overall stature of the man and the roll of his shoulders when he walked: he knew it to be the cowboy with the long moustache. Charlie was surprised to find that the man wasn't holding a gun.

'I apologize for the unorthodox manner of our meeting,' he said. 'My name is Tom Chisum, I'm a Texas Ranger.'

'You were Clem Cole's partner!'

'That's right. I guess he was looking for me the day he was killed.'

'You were at the Sutton ranch.'

'Yes. Like Clem I was using an assumed name and I couldn't admit knowing him. It was obvious that he'd been identified and it was possible that you were his killer.'

'What makes you think differently now?'

'I know you. I thought I recognized you out at the Sutton spread, but it wasn't until I heard the deputy announce that you'd been working with the army that I was sure.'

'We've met before?' asked Charlie.

Tom Chisum's grin contained a stiff measure of ironic humour. 'Our paths have crossed but we haven't been formally introduced.'

Charlie understood his meaning: they'd been adversaries during his days spent chasing those Rebel bands that had refused to admit the war was over. Charlie inspected the other's face to determine if revenge for earlier events was in his mind, but after a moment he dismissed that thought. Not every gang had been seeking personal gain: for some it was still the belief that their state had prospered better before the war and they wanted a return to those days. So, if now that it was clear that the Union could not be overthrown Tom Chisum had chosen to serve his state as a Ranger, then Charlie had no cause for argument. Furthermore, he was no longer acting on behalf of the government, so he was happy for bygones to be bygones.

'Your message was that you had some information for me.'

'Yes, it was, but I was hoping that we might be able to help each other.'

Charlie didn't see how that could be possible; the only help he needed was in finding his old saddle. The death of Harker meant that its location would never be discovered, and he had no information that would help the Texas Rangers to catch their man.

'I'm only here because someone stole my horse. That man is now dead, so I'll be moving on as soon as possible.'

'What about Farraday?' asked Chisum. 'Aren't you interested in finding him?'

'No,' Charlie said, but that was only partly true. If those men who had attacked him that morning had been obeying Farraday's orders, then he would like to meet him face to face. 'I'd never heard of him before yesterday.'

Chisum persisted. 'He swindled money from the town of Johnson City and two men were killed when pursuing him. All over Texas there are Rangers on the lookout for him, anxious to stop him pulling something similar in another town. By taking jobs, Clem and I hoped to be able to learn of any unusual activities here in Mortimer without arousing suspicion.'

'What did you discover?'

'I hadn't discovered anything, but I reckon Clem must have been on to something; he had no other reason to be seeking me out at the Sutton place.'

'Whatever he learned got him killed,' said Charlie.

'And if it is proved that Farraday had a hand in the murder of a Ranger it will increase the reward for his capture.'

A glint showed in Tom Chisum's eyes, as though the mention of money would be attractive to Charlie. Charlie could understand why he would think that. As a government agent he'd earned a fee for capturing Rebels and breaking up the gangs, but Charlie had seen that as helping to bring peace to the Southern states at the end of the war, not bounty hunting. Ordinarily, he would have rejected Chisum's suggestion out of hand, but now he was penniless and the prospect of a hundred dollars or more was a temptation.

'I don't know how I can help,' he said. 'I wouldn't know the man Farraday if I passed him in the street.'

'But he knows you, or someone close to him does. He must have set those gunmen on to you this morning, don't you think? Just keep doing what you've been doing and I reckon he'll come looking for you again.'

Charlie had to admit that he had no other enemies in Mortimer, but Chisum's scheme seemed like an open invitation for Farraday to find and kill him.

'Offer myself up as a sacrificial goat?' he said.

'I'll be shadowing you. Nobody knows I'm anything other than a dusty trail-hand.'

Charlie couldn't forget that Tom Chisum had been a member of one of the Rebel gangs he'd chased. It was possible that what he was suggesting was nothing more than a means to exact revenge.

105

'So I'll get shot and you'll get the man and the reward.'

Tom Chisum's face hardened. 'I'm a Texas Ranger; we can't claim rewards for the criminals we capture, but Clem Cole was my partner and I don't intend to let his murder go unpunished. I'd appreciate your help. If you don't give it then I'll find Farraday without you.'

The earnestness of Chisum's response impressed Charlie but still he shook his head. 'It's none of my affair.'

'It became your affair when you found Clem Cole.'

Charlie corrected him. 'I didn't find Clem Cole.'

'But you were with him when he died and you heard his last words.' An attempted interruption by Charlie was drowned out by more words from Chisum. 'You're the sort of man around whom things happen, Mr Jefferson. I know that Farraday will be flushed out if you hang around town.'

To himself Charlie admitted that there needed to be a personal reckoning with Farraday, who had unleashed gunmen against him with orders to kill, but he wasn't yet prepared to fall in with Chisum's scheme.

'I'll think about it,' he said, as he walked away, out through the high main doors into the sunlight.

Disappointed by Charlie Jefferson's lack of enthusiasm, Tom Chisum lingered in the stable to nullify the risk that they would be seen together by anyone who had not been drawn to the riverside. He allowed a minute to pass, then he, too, headed for the high doors. In a nearby stall a horse shuffled nervously and snickered. Chisum paused, threw a few gentling words to the horse as he passed, then stopped. Sunlight was pouring into the stable from the now open doors and he could see that the horse was in full harness. Curious, because unsaddling animals that are housed in the livery is always the first task of the stableman, Tom Chisum stopped at the stall.

Stretching out a hand he rubbed the horse's face. It was cool, which meant that it hadn't recently arrived in town and been left by its rider to be tended to when Gus Brewer returned. The horse shook its head so that the head-harness rattled, and this was answered by a similar sound from across the aisle. Surprised to know that a second horse in the stable was saddled, Tom Chisum turned to examine it.

A figure in black emerged from the box, partially crouched, in a fighting stance, and instantly Tom saw the gleam from a long knife blade. His first instinct was to go for the pistol at his side, but the man lunged and Tom had to take evasive action to prevent the knife slicing into his stomach. He backed away but soon came up against the timber wall of a stall. His opponent came at him again, almost jumping into this attack, giving Tom no time to reach for his gun, no alternative but to try to

107

block the thrust, grab for the wrist holding the knife and turn it away from his body.

But the man in black was strong and had the benefit of surprise on his side. For a few seconds they grappled, Tom using both hands to hold the wrist that held the weapon. With his free fist, his left, Sol Barclay landed a blow on the Ranger's jaw, causing him to stagger, tipping him sideways, forcing him down on to one knee. Shaken, Tom Chisum's instinct was to grip more tightly the hand that held the knife. Barclay tried hard to free himself from that grip and lashed out again at Tom Chisum's head. This time, however, his intention was obvious and even though Tom was still recovering from the first blow he was able to avoid the full impact by dropping below the trajectory of the swipe and taking the blow on the top of his head.

Barclay attacked again, using his free hand to grab one of Tom's wrists and using his superior strength to free himself from the restraining grip. He swung the knife in a deadly arc and Tom had to slither across the floor to avoid it. But it was a temporary escape. Sol Barclay leapt full length, crashing his body into Tom's, pinning him to the ground. Once again he raised the knife, expecting to end the fight by plunging it into the other's heart.

But Tom wasn't yet beaten. He had survived the war and survived the aftermath, neither of which had been achieved by being a pacifist so, although this assault had taken him completely by surprise, he had reserves of fighting knowledge to call upon. With the weight of Sol Barclay upon him it seemed that he was completely trapped; however, his right arm was free and although he had little room in which to build up momentum, he still managed to land a punch on the point of Barclay's chin before the knife descended.

It wasn't the most powerful blow Tom had ever thrown or the most powerful that Sol had ever taken, but it was enough to dislodge the black-garbed assailant and allow Tom to kick himself free. He scrambled to his feet and staggered towards the open door, struggling to pull his pistol from its holster. But Barclay came at him again, swinging with the knife which sliced Tom's forearm, forcing him to shout with pain and drop his gun.

With that success Sol went for the kill, slashing a wicked line across Tom's body from his left shoulder almost to his waist. Tom screamed and fell to the ground. For a brief moment Sol Barclay stood over him, considered stabbing again to ensure the Ranger would never recover, but decided that he needed to be away while there was no one around to witness his departure. Sol turned to collect the horses from the stable, which he then quit through the back door.

Fighting to the last, Tom Chisum's now bloody fingers reached for the pistol that was lying on the ground. Weakened by pain and loss of blood, he could barely raise the piece or aim it when he did, but he pulled the trigger and the shot hurried Sol Barclay on his way. He had to get clear before anyone saw him and observed the direction in which he'd fled.

Charlie Jefferson had walked three blocks along Main Street when he saw the first people swarming back to town from the riverside. At the same moment he heard the gunshot behind him and stopped in his tracks. He knew that it could only have come from one place: the stable he had just left, so he ran back in that direction.

Tom was face down in the dust. When Charlie raised and turned him he emitted a dreadful groan.

'Who was it, Tom?' asked Charlie.

With difficulty, the Ranger opened his eyes and it was clear that he recognized Charlie Jefferson. He gripped his arm.

'He heard us,' he whispered.

'There was someone else in the stable?' Tom's head moved in a slight nod of confirmation. 'Was it Farraday?'

'No. Someone in black.'

'Where did he go?'

'Horses. Back door,' Chisum managed to say before passing out.

By then other townsmen had arrived and Charlie ordered someone to get a doctor while he went through the stables to the corrals at the rear in the hope of catching a glimpse of Tom Chisum's attacker. But he wasn't in sight and there were too many horse-tracks to know which way he'd gone.

CHAPTER TEN

Many people along the river bank had greeted Sammy Sutton during the afternoon, and she had spent time gossiping with the girls she knew and exchanging greetings with those older citizens who had been friends of her family for most of her life. Dave Champion, who knew less than a handful of people in Mortimer, was her constant companion and together they watched the major events, each having selected a favourite to win and both being wrong every time.

Much against her father's wishes Sammy had brought her pinto to town with the intention of racing her. She was a swift animal and Samantha enjoyed nothing better than galloping her over the open range land around the ranch house. Her father had warned her that racing was a different matter, that riders got up to all sorts of tricks in an effort to win and he knew that her youth and sex were unlikely to gain her any consideration.

However, when the time came to enrol, the elation with which she had been filled earlier that morning had evaporated and she no longer had the desire to test the filly against the best in that corner of Texas.

It was Charlie Jefferson's cold response to her invitation to share the afternoon with her and Dave that had sapped the girl's spirit. She had thought of little else but the tall cowboy since he had first answered her call for assistance as she tended the dying man near her home, but twice he had spurned her, dismissing her as though she was nothing more than an irritating schoolgirl.

The sensation she had experienced when he'd first knelt at her side was something she'd not known before. It wasn't as though she'd never been alone with a man: she had been accompanied by several of the ranch hands when riding into Mortimer or across to the relay station where the Champions lived. Some had talked seriously and some had teased her but none at parting had made her fear that she might not see them again. Despite his scarcely speaking a word, that was the effect that Charlie Jefferson had had on her. She had raced home for the flat wagon and had insisted on accompanying Buck back to the scene of the shooting, desperate to return in case the shot man had died and Charlie had ridden away.

Later, at the ranch, he hadn't been in awe of her father as many were, but had spoken to him like a man who expected to be listened to, not impolite or

113

demanding, but expecting respect and answers to the questions he posed. Perhaps he'd been rough with Eli Ringwood but Eli had been astride Charlie's stolen horse and it was clear that Charlie wouldn't rest until he had caught up with the thief. The fact that when he had done so he'd had to spend the night in jail was testament to the fact that he was a man prepared to back up his words with action. Sammy had been annoyed to learn that he'd been in the cells overnight, and after she and her father had confirmed his story she had demanded his immediate release.

Then the sheriff had been killed. When she realized that Charlie had no means of defending himself she had thought her heart would stop. She could barely remember climbing on to her pony or how she had managed to get the rifle to Charlie with which he killed his attackers. What she did remember were the moments afterwards, when she was pressed against his chest and his arms were around her shoulders. Despite her father's later rant at the foolishness of her action she knew she would do the same again in similar circumstances.

Yet now Charlie was cool towards her, almost anxious to be distant from her. She didn't understand it and she couldn't stop thinking about him.

If Sammy's regular periods of preoccupation were noted by Dave Champion he didn't remark on them; he was somewhat overawed by the occasion and was having great fun. This was Mortimer's first Founding Day celebration since the end of the war and therefore the first one that Dave had attended. He had never seen so many laughing and smiling people, nor heard so much good-natured bragging as that resorted to by the entrants to the various competitions. He entered into the spirit of the occasion with gusto, took part in a sack race and tried his hand at pole-climbing but didn't come close to winning either contest.

For the rest of the afternoon he found appropriate vantage points where he and Sammy could watch the races and any other events that caught their fancy. He yelled encouragement as loud as anyone but his favourite moment was watching a bunch of cowboys trying to catch a greased pig, which ran and squealed as it eluded their efforts. Their futile antics caused great hilarity among those gathered around. Two of the cowboys worked at the Sutton ranch and their inept efforts to hang on to the wriggling animal brought a smile to Sammy's face, forced her, for a moment, to forget about Charlie Jefferson.

Most families had brought picnic baskets and several of those with whom Sammy was familiar shared their cakes and pies with her and Dave, but there were also stalls selling popcorn, taffy and drinks. It was when Dave had been to buy lemonade for Sammy and himself with some of the coins his father had pushed into his pocket before leaving home, that the disaster occurred.

That morning, a team of well-meaning townsmen had almost completed assembling the viewing stand when they learned of the killing of Sheriff Agnew. One of the men was married to the sheriff's sister. Anxious to be with her when she learned of Abe's death, he failed to properly secure the final brackets that fixed the planks to the poles. The stand was big enough to hold more than 200 people but not until this moment, when the final race of the day was about to begin, had it been required to bear anything close to its full capacity. Now, it was crowded and people were moving on every level, trying to get the best possible view as race time approached. Although the fastenings had held throughout the afternoon, the constant tread of spectators had loosened them to such an extent that now, under full stress, the boards under the feet of the crowd were beginning to sway.

Dave had left Sammy at the back of the five-tier-high stand and when he reached the foot of it with a glass of lemonade in each hand he wondered how he would ever get to her before the race began. He was standing at the corner, looking up, when two of the end poles collapsed and the nearest boards and the people on them began to fall.

Chaos ensued. The crashing sounds of timber was accompanied by the shouts of those men and women who were affected and who were tumbling or jumping to the ground. Fearing that the whole stand was on the point of collapse, the remaining spectators tried to get clear, those at the back pushing those in front, causing pandemonium to spread right along the river bank. There was much noise, much panic and a great loss of dignity as several men and women emerged with torn and dirty clothing.

Only one person received any serious injury. Dave Champion was struck on the head by one of the falling planks. Knocked senseless, he was covered by debris then crushed under the bodies of the dislodged people. By the time some kind of order was restored he was completely hidden and when he was discovered the immediate assumption was that he was dead.

Dr Alan Spenser, who had been tending to the minor bumps and bruises of those who considered their tumble deserved some sort of attention, was summoned and he reached Dave at the same time as Sammy Sutton. She had searched the riverbank for her young friend and was almost distraught when the news reached her that he had been killed. However, although the boy was still unconscious and his face was covered with blood, he was alive but his breathing was raspy and uneven. To examine him properly Dr Spenser had Dave Champion carried to his home. Sammy went with them.

It was there, with the boy cleaned up, bandaged and sleeping, that Horry Blackmore found the doctor and told him there had been a stabbing incident down at Gus Brewer's stable. Leaving Sammy to sit with Dave, Spenser grabbed his medical bag and hurried down the street.

In the absence of clean linen, Gus Brewer had suggested that a wadding of straw should be applied to the long gash in Tom Chisum's chest, but by the time Dr Spenser got to the wounded man several handfuls had become saturated with blood. After a quick examination the doctor berated those standing around.

'You men should have got him to my house. I can't do anything for him on this dusty street.'

Nobody argued; everyone knew it was one of those situations when they were likely to be wrong whichever course of action they took. If they'd carried Tom Chisum down to the doctor's house and he'd died en route the doctor would have said he should have been left where he fell until he'd had the opportunity to examine him. But now, following the doctor's grumble, they reacted quickly. A suitable piece of wood to serve as a stretcher was brought from inside the stable and they loaded the wounded man on to it.

Walking side by side with the doctor in the wake of the bearers, Charlie asked about the Ranger's chances of survival.

'Can't say until I know how deep the knife reached and what organs have been damaged,' he was told, 'but the man's lost a lot of blood, which

118

alone can be fatal.' The doctor peered at Charlie. 'Who are you?' he asked.

'The name is Charlie Jefferson.'

Dr Spenser moved his head in a swift, curt nod. 'Thought it might be. Sheriff Agnew got killed because of you and now more violence. What's going on? You trying to turn this place into a ghost town?'

Charlie didn't respond to that. 'That man's a Texas Ranger,' he informed the doctor, 'and what happened to him is due to his efforts to protect this town. Do what you can for him.'

The doctor answered sharply. 'I do what I can for everyone who comes under my care.'

By this time they'd reached the doctor's home and Tom Chisum was carried inside.

At the door, Charlie said, 'I'd like to call by later to see how he's doing.'

'Can't promise he'll be able to talk to anyone.'

Charlie wasn't sure if the doctor's discouraging response was professional caution or a personal rebuff. He was about to press the man again but decided that it was imperative for Tom Chisum to receive the doctor's total attention. He was about to leave when a movement in another room caught his eye and suddenly Samantha Sutton was before him. Briefly, they exchanged details of the events that had brought them together at the home of the doctor and Charlie voiced his concern when Samantha told him about the collapse of the stand

and the injury to Dave Champion. He was no less anxious to learn if she had been hurt and was relieved by her assurance that, as she had been at the other end of the stand, she had been unaffected by the turmoil.

'I'll wait here until Dave is awake,' she told him. 'The doctor thinks he'll be well enough to travel later. There is a stagecoach leaving here in a couple of hours which will take him home. Travelling in that will be more comfortable than my father's buggy. I'll travel with him then ride back to the ranch after he's settled at home with his father.'

At that moment, her father was sitting in a room in the courthouse alongside Mayor Baker, the Templeton brothers and Oliver Calloway. The purpose of the meeting had been to calculate the total amount that would be passed on to Thomas Cartwright now that those citizens willing to participate in the scheme to bring a branch-line to Mortimer had had the opportunity to hand over their money. Those donations together with the more substantial sums contributed by the town treasury, the Templetons, Henry Sutton, and Oliver Calloway by proxy for the bank were being counted in another room while these men drank brandy and puffed cigars. But what should have been a meeting of some celebration now had an air of edginess to it as the events of the afternoon, the collapse of the viewing stand and the knifing at Gus Brewer's stable came under discussion.

'How will Thomas Cartwright react if he learns of these events?' asked Joel Templeton. 'Will he still be prepared to support our enterprise?'

'I thought he was showing reluctance after the shooting of Abe Agnew,' his brother said. 'He thought the railroad company would frown on a disorderly town.'

'And now there's been a public disaster. The directors aren't likely to invest in a town that can't look after its own citizens,' warned Oliver Calloway.

'Perhaps Cartwright won't tell them,' said Dustin Baker. 'Perhaps he hasn't heard the news. I do believe he intended spending the afternoon in his room, resting for the journey ahead.'

'It's possible, I suppose,' mused Curt Templeton. 'I suggest we don't say anything. Just hand over the money and get him out of town quickly. Once he's accepted our money there will be no turning back. Even if later he hears about the collapse of the stand it is unlikely that he'll pass on the details to the directors of the railroad. I don't doubt that he gains financially when they adopt his proposal so he won't want Gatling to win the prize.'

There were murmurs of agreement around the room and at that moment the two men who had been acting as tellers in the outer chamber entered. The sum of money they'd packed and locked into large carpetbag was a little over $40,000, a paltry amount compared to the proposed first instalment of $200,000, but Oliver Calloway was certain that the bank would give them huge financial support once it was agreed that the branch-line would be built.

'Come then, gentlemen,' said Mayor Baker, 'let us deliver this money to Mr Cartwright and we'll urge Harry Goater at the stage office to get the coach ready to travel as soon as possible. We've messed about with its departure time for the sake of Founder's Day, but now that the events are ended there is no reason to delay it any longer.'

Harry Goater insisted that the coach would leave at the rescheduled time and not a moment before. By the time someone was sent to summon both driver and guard it would barely bring departure time forward by thirty minutes and, as the coach was only going as far as John Champion's relay station that night, it wasn't worth the bother.

Mayor Baker didn't like having his authority opposed but Curt Templeton was of the opinion that changing the departure time might make Thomas Cartwright think they were keen to get him out of town, so it was almost two hours later when they assembled at the stage depot to usher Thomas Cartwright into the coach along with his baggage, which included the carpetbag full of money. When the coach pulled away the members of the town council exchanged smiles and back-slaps, confident that they had secured a railway link for Mortimer which, in turn, would provide a boost to their own ambitions and finances.

To Thomas Cartwright's surprise the coach rolled along the street at little more than walking pace. When it came to a halt he thrust his head out of the window to ask the driver for an explanation.

'Someone to collect,' he was told and though he blustered that he had been assured that he was the only passenger, no one took any notice of him.

Charlie Jefferson tied Samantha Sutton's pinto to the back of the coach, then went into the doctor's house to collect Dave Champion. He carried him out wrapped in a thick grey blanket and put him on the long seat opposite Cartwright.

'What's wrong with him?' Cartwright demanded. 'Is he diseased?' His face showed his distaste for sharing with someone in ill health.

'He's had an accident,' Charlie told him. 'He's going home.'

Cartwright was going to continue his protest but one look at Charlie's face hushed the words. Then Samantha Sutton climbed into the coach and his countenance altered. It was a change of expression which didn't escape Charlie's notice. He took in the man's features, the fair, curly hair and mutton-chop sideburns, the heavy-lidded dark-blue eyes and the prominent Roman nose. He was a big man, heavy, but good clothes managed to hide the fact that his bulk was not all hard muscle.

'I'll ride out tomorrow,' Charlie told the girl, making the words a clear warning to the passenger.

At that moment, Henry Sutton, who had joined his daughter at the doctor's house after the meeting at the courthouse, looked into the coach with some final words for Sammy.

'Stay overnight with the Champions if it gets too dark to travel. John will find a room for you.' Then he saw the man in the opposite corner. 'Cartwright,' he acknowledged. 'Safe journey.' Then the door was closed and the driver yelled at the horses and slapped the leathers on their flanks. The coach pulled away and Charlie Jefferson and Henry Sutton watched it until it was out of sight.

'Who was that man?' asked Charlie.

'Thomas Cartwright. He's an important man to this town. Through him, Mortimer is about to prosper.'

Henry Sutton didn't say any more; he wasn't forgetting that Charlie Jefferson was just passing through the territory and until the railroad announced the construction of a spur line it was better to restrict knowledge of it to those it affected. Nor was he forgetting that the recent acts of violence had occurred after Charlie Jefferson's arrival.

Charlie wasn't interested in the man's business dealings; he was concerned by the animal look that had flashed across Cartwright's face when he saw Samantha. He consoled himself with the fact that Samantha and Dave were only travelling as far as the first relay station. He didn't know that the coach was stopping there overnight and he might not have given the fancifully dressed man another thought if, two hours later, Horry Blackmore hadn't joined him at a table in the Rose of Texas.

The deputy looked uncomfortable, as though he had something on his mind, something for which he would be blamed and didn't know how to rid himself of the problem.

'Another telegraph message for the sheriff,' he began, mumbling, turning his head this way and that to make sure that no one was listening. 'From the Texas Rangers' office in Austin.' He looked around again. 'It seems that Sheriff Agnew made an enquiry about the man called Farraday.'

'What did the reply say?'

'That he is wanted for fraud and murder. A poster was issued about him nine months ago.'

'Have you found it?'

Horry nodded and reached inside his shirt for the large sheet of paper that had been twice folded. He moved closer to Charlie in order to confine sight of the picture to the two of them. It was a scratchy drawing as, in Charlie's experience, all such posters were, but when he saw it Charlie immediately knew the face. The features depicted showed a prominent nose and big, heavy-lidded eyes, a large face topped with curly hair.

'Do you know this man?' Charlie asked Horry.

Horry nodded. 'He calls himself Thomas Cartwright and he's taken the town's money to bring the railroad to Mortimer.'

125

'What?'

'What should I do?'

'You need to wire ahead to the next town that the coach reaches and have the sheriff there arrest him.'

When Horry informed him that the coach was travelling only as far as Champion's relay station that night, Charlie's thoughts immediately centred on Samantha Sutton and the possibility that she, too, might stay overnight at the relay station. He remembered the feral look that had crossed Cartwright/Farraday's face as Samantha settled herself in the coach beside Dave Champion. Abruptly he stood, determined to ride out to the relay station even though twilight was almost upon them.

Horry grabbed his sleeve. 'What should I do? he asked again.

'Tell the mayor what has happened, then organize a posse and get out to John Champion's relay station as quickly as possible. You can't let him escape.'

CHAPTER ELEVEN

Dave Champion didn't react well to the lurching, swaying movement of the coach. Doctor Spenser had warned him that the journey would be unpleasant and that he'd rather keep him under observation for the night, but the hours of rest on the doctor's couch had subdued the pain in Dave's head and lulled the lad into believing that the worst was over. The prospect of being at home with his father was worth a little discomfort. But the combination of ragged motion and the persistent sounds generated by horses, coach and driver were sufficient to arouse once more the sensations of pain and nausea from which he thought he'd escaped. Before they were halfway to the relay station his face had become drained of all colour and his eyes were tightly closed in an effort to fight the pain in his head.

Concerned for her young friend, Sammy Sutton tucked the blanket around him and pressed her cool hand against his forehead. He was hot but he shivered, and when the right front wheel struck a rock causing that corner of the coach to lift then bounce on landing, he moaned loudly. The doctor had supplied a cushion for the journey which Sammy now adjusted under the lad's head in an effort to make him more comfortable.

Thomas Cartwright was talking to her, as he had tried to do with little success for most of the journey. Sammy had answered his initial enquiries and observations with politeness but she soon became uncomfortable with his conversation, and as Dave's need of her attention grew the easier it was to ignore the dandy fellow, which was what she was doing now while considering means of reducing Dave's discomfort.

Henry Sutton had built up his ranch by means of his own hard work and although he was now able to employ men to work with the stock and in all other aspects of managing the business, it didn't mean that he no longer engaged in those tasks himself, nor did it mean that his daughter didn't get her hands dirty. Perhaps it would have been different if Sammy hadn't been such a tomboy, but she worked cattle and helped to maintain the property as eagerly as her father and as well as any of the hired hands. Consequently, agile and stronger than her slim frame suggested, she had the utmost confidence in her own abilities, often surprising people with undertakings that no one would suspect her capable of achieving.

So it was now. With a supple twist of her shoulders she eased her way through the narrow side-opening. Then, reaching up to grip the metal containing-rail on the roof of the coach, she pulled herself through until she was able to stand on the bottom ledge of the opening. With head and shoulders above the top of the coach, she called to the driver, needing to shout to make herself heard above the rumble of the wheels, Tex's commands to the horses and the occasional crack of the whip.

'Get back inside,' Tex Hames told her when he recovered from his initial surprise. 'Are you trying to kill yourself?'

'Slow down,' she told him, explaining that Dave was ill and as they were only going as far as the relay station there was no reason to race the horses.

Tex grumbled that he was in charge and that he wouldn't do anything until she got back inside, but already he was pulling on the long leathers to control the speed of his team.

When she slipped the lower half of her body back into the coach, Thomas Cartwright placed his hands around her waist and held her as if to support and guide her to safety.

'Allow me,' he said.

Uncomfortable at his touch, Sammy shrugged to dislodge his hold, then pushed at his hands.

'I'm fine,' she said.

'I'm impressed,' he said, his hands still on her

129

hips. 'That was quite a feat.'

Sammy placed her hands on his chest and pushed. He stumbled, perhaps due to the swaying of the coach, and sat down heavily on his seat. A grin spread across his face. It unnerved Sammy, and as she retook her place at Dave Champion's side she wondered if asking Tex Hames to slow down had been a mistake.

John Champion had been watching for the arrival of the coach for more than an hour when it eventually appeared, travelling so sedately that he figured one of the horses had cast a shoe or strained a tendon, and so the driver was nursing it to the relay station where it could be doctored before morning.

'Your boy's inside,' Tex told him as he brought the team to a standstill. 'There's been an accident.'

Sammy told Dave's father what had happened while he carried his pale and bandaged son into the house. Anxious to learn the full extent of his son's injuries, John Champion neglected his duty and left the horses harnessed to the coach. He told Tex Hames and Barnaby Coutts, the shotgun guard, to help themselves to coffee. Thomas Cartwright, keeping a tight hold on the carpetbag, which had travelled with him inside the coach, sat at the communal table. He was hungry and anxious to have his stomach filled in preparation for the travelling he planned to undertake when darkness fell.

A regular running of the journey from Mortimer

to the Champions' stage depot would have meant that Sammy Sutton would have mounted her pinto and ridden home before darkness fell, but because of the slow pace, it had been almost twilight before they reached their destination. Reluctant to leave until she was sure that her young friend was settled, she unhitched the pinto from the back of the coach and led him to a water trough at the rear of the building. Darkness fell suddenly in that part of the country and Sammy soon realized that she would need to stay at the relay station for the night.

John Champion allotted one of the rooms to her but after she'd eaten and helped him to wash the dishes, she went to sit with Dave and was there until the lad fell asleep. Sitting in Dave's room wasn't without an ulterior motive. Thomas Cartwright had cast sly looks in her direction while everyone had been gathered around the table, and she wasn't eager to spend any great length of time in his company.

In fact, Cartwright had taken to his own room shortly after the meal, anxious to grab a little sleep before Sol Barclay arrived with the horses. Over a pack of cards and a bottle of whiskey, the stage crew, Tex and Barnaby, brought John Champion up to date with affairs in Mortimer and other towns along the stage routes. So it was late when the last light was extinguished and silence settled around the low buildings of the relay station.

When a day is full of events such as those that had

filled Sammy Sutton's day the result is either a night
of deep, satisfying sleep or a sleepless night. This
night, for Sammy, it was the latter. Over and over,
she recalled her arrival in town to learn of Charlie
Jefferson's arrest, followed by the ambush attempt
which had resulted in the death of Sheriff Agnew
rather than Charlie's, and then the collapse of the
stand which, momentarily, she thought had ended
Dave Champion's life. She had been relieved to discover that he had not been killed; so much so that
she had served as his nurse for the remainder of the
day.

Now she should be sleeping but the thoughts in
her mind were too vivid, especially when she tried
to understand the behaviour of Charlie Jefferson.
He was a puzzle: at one moment shunning her and
then showing genuine concern for her safety when
he thought that she, too, might have been injured
when the viewing stand collapsed. With a sigh,
Sammy got off the bunk and went outside to seek
the company of her pinto who was in the corral at
the side of the house.

From his position on a high southern ridge, Sol
Barclay had seen the arrival of the coach and had
settled down to wait for darkness. When, at last, no
more lights showed from the buildings, he saddled
the two horses and set off to the rendezvous. To give
those within the station time to settle into sleep,
and so as not to cause any unnecessary noise, he

walked the last half-mile. When he reached the yard he halted, unsure what signal to give to let Cartwright know he'd arrived.

As it happened, none was necessary. In a moment, a figure emerged from the darkness of the doorway and his bulk made his identity unmistakable. Barclay grinned when he saw the carpetbag that Cartwright clutched to his chest. Wordlessly, Cartwright took the proffered reins and the two men turned to lead the horses to a distance far enough from the house for the sound of their hoof beats not to awaken those sleeping within.

Suddenly a voice carried across the yard. A female voice that was full of suspicion.

'What are you doing?' called Sammy.

The unexpected challenge brought about different reactions. Barclay, thinking only of escape, drew his pistol and would have fired at the girl, but Cartwright grabbed his arm before the gun was fully clear of the holster.

'A bonus,' he hissed. 'She's the daughter of a local landowner. He'll pay for her return.'

'Are you crazy?' snarled Barclay. 'We can't hang around for ransom money. Let's go with what we've got before the house is aroused.'

But talk of a ransom was just an excuse that had leapt into Cartwright's mind; he knew that a demand for money would never be made, but the young girl's sudden appearance presented him with an opportunity that he couldn't resist. Throughout the coach ride from Mortimer she had aroused an immediate need in him, one he intended to fulfil at the earliest opportunity.

Having dropped the reins he'd been given, he was already striding across the yard towards Sammy Sutton, a smile on his face that was hidden in the darkness and words on his lips that kept her silent while she listened to his explanation.

'Many people in Mortimer know I'm carrying a lot of money,' he said, his voice low but distinct. 'It's necessary to take precautions.'

By now he was only half a dozen steps from Sammy and the look on his face startled her. She backed away, but with unexpected suddenness Cartwright lunged for her, his right hand reaching out to get a grip around her mouth and prevent her from shouting out an alarm.

Sammy, although surprised by the attack, was not so easily caught. Again she sprang backwards so that his grasp missed its target but filled itself with her shirt. She shouted in alarm and her pinto, startled by the quick movements, jumped and gave a loud whinny. Sol Barclay's voice carried across the yard, urging Cartwright to climb on to his horse and forget the girl. They had money to share and if they stuck to their plan they would be out of Texas before anyone knew they'd been robbed.

'Come on,' he shouted as he climbed into the saddle. Realizing his raised voice might have aroused those in the relay station he drew his gun and covered the door.

Meanwhile Cartwright had dragged the girl towards him. She kicked his shins, hurt him, and called out again for help from the house. The unsettled pinto had disturbed the other animals in the corral and they were milling around, snorting, stamping, rearing and snickering like there was a wolf in their midst.

From the house sounds of activity could be heard, and somewhere there was the butterfly flicker of light from a candle. Once again Sol Barclay called for Cartwright to escape with the money and leave the girl but the big man wasn't prepared to accept that he couldn't have both. Holding the bag of money in his left hand he made a final effort. He pulled the girl forward with his right hand, then, releasing his grip on her clothing, formed that same hand into a fist and punched her on the jaw. Although Sammy had been moving away from the impact it still carried enough power to stun her. Her knees sagged and she would have fallen to the ground if Cartwright hadn't caught her.

Using mainly his right arm, he dragged her across the yard to where Sol Barclay waited. He lifted Sammy and threw her across the saddle in front of Sol, causing the horse to jerk away, performing a half-circle with a series of short, nervous steps.

Cartwright caught hold of the trailing rein

attached to his own horse and, using the wooden handles on the top, hung the carpetbag over the saddle horn. With one foot in a stirrup, he was preparing to mount when the door of the relay station opened and John Champion, rifle at the ready, came out to investigate.

'Who's there?' he demanded.

Cartwright tried the same explanation on John Champion that he'd tried a few moments earlier with Sammy Sutton. He might have got away with it if Sol's skittish horse hadn't felt the need to perform another nervous turn. That was when John saw the bundle across Sol's saddle and even in the darkness of the night the yellow shirt stood out like signal flag.

'Hey,' he called, 'is that Sammy?'

Sol Barclay, experienced in the execution of a crime, had kept his pistol in his hand although, until this moment, it had been hidden from John Champion. Now he raised it and without warning fired. John Champion staggered backwards and fell into the house. Barnaby Coutts, roused from a whiskey-influenced slumber, reached the doorway some seconds later. He fired one of the barrels of his shotgun at the fleeing horsemen, but by then they were out of range and riding hell for leather for the high ground.

CHAPTER TWELVE

No more than ten minutes passed between the departure of Thomas Cartwright and Sol Barclay and the dust-raising arrival of Charlie Jefferson. From afar and unexpectedly, flickers of light had directed him to the relay station. As he drew closer he could pick out lamp-carrying figures in the yard. A gut feeling told him that a stealthy approach was unnecessary, that the activity had been instigated by Farraday, the object of his pursuit.

Just as the lamplight had guided him to his destination, so the noise of his approach had carried like a clarion note in the stillness of the night. When he pulled the sweating gelding to an abrupt, stone-scattering halt, he found himself facing the long barrels of a shotgun. His challenger's voice came gruffly through the darkness, like that of a man surprised by his own nervousness.

'Who's there?'

'My name's Charlie Jefferson. I'm seeking a man

called Farraday who was a passenger on the stage from Mortimer.' Charlie knew he had the wrong name, couldn't remember the one that Farraday was currently using, but didn't figure it would matter.

'Jefferson,' repeated Barnaby Coutts, clearly recalling events in Mortimer. 'He's gone,' he added, 'him and another fellow shot John Champion and skedaddled before I could get a good shot at them.

Charlie jumped down from his weary, foam-flecked horse. 'Is he shot bad?'

'Bad enough. Hit high on the chest and the slug is still in him. Tex and me got him inside but neither of us has the skill to do more. I was just picking out a horse to ride for a doctor.'

Charlie turned towards the house. 'Is he conscious?'

'Barely.' Barnaby Coutts didn't know whether to stick to the task of saddling a horse or follow Charlie inside.

'Anyone else injured?'

'No. Like I told you, they were out of range before I could get a clean shot at them.'

Inside the house, Charlie found John Champion lying on the long table covered with a thin blanket. Tex Hames was hovering, ill at ease, near by. Tex held up a lamp to get a better look at the new arrival and blurted out that he'd been woken by the gunshot, as though suspecting he was going to be blamed for what had happened.

Charlie glanced around, surprised that Samantha wasn't in attendance, then he felt a rush of relief as he assumed she'd gone back to the Sutton ranch before the violence had erupted.

'Where's the boy?' he asked.

'Dave had a rough journey. I reckon he's still a-bed.'

'He doesn't know his pa's been shot?'

Tex shook his head. 'Should we tell him?'

'No.' The word was little more than a croak uttered by John Champion whose eyes were now open. His hand was reaching for Charlie's arm. 'It'll keep until the morning,' he said, his determination to prove that that was true brightening his eyes.

'Take it easy,' said Charlie, 'we'll get a doctor here as soon as possible.'

'That's not important,' John Champion replied. 'You've got to get Sammy back.'

John Champion's meaning was misunderstood by Charlie who thought the relay station manager wanted Samantha to be brought back from the Sutton spread.

'No,' hissed the depot manager, 'they took her. That's why they shot me. She was slung unconscious over one of the horses.'

The news spurred Charlie into immediate action, questioning the others as to which direction the abductors had fled.

'They were riding south, towards the high ground,' Barnaby Coutts told him. 'Of course, once they were swallowed by the darkness they could have gone in any direction.'

'If I'm to catch them I'll need a fresh horse,' Charlie declared. This time he wouldn't tolerate a refusal, for the reason that they were company animals in the corral.

But John Champion surprised him, pulled him close, made himself heard despite his laboured breathing.

'Take Sammy's pinto,' he told Charlie. 'That filly is a racer. It's sure to outrun them.'

Charlie agreed. If one of the horses was carrying double they wouldn't be able to maintain a great pace for long. He darted for the corral, switched his saddle on to the pinto and was off towards the high country within minutes.

For a second time Sol Barclay pulled his horse to a halt. Progress had been slow, not only because the uneven terrain was making it difficult to set a sustained pace, but because conscious, the girl was a nuisance, wriggling and kicking, twisting and shouting, forcing him to attend to her objections rather than concentrate on putting miles between themselves and the stage station. As with many men, the war had left him with few morals. He had killed, robbed and cheated without qualms since enlisting in 1861 and now, eight years later, he was wanted in four states and faced a death sentence in two of those. But, despite his reckless reputation and despite possessing the survival cunning with which men of his kind are often endowed, Sol Barclay knew that to maintain his freedom it was imperative to avoid unnecessary risks. Kidnapping girls, he knew, was the greatest unnecessary risk of all. A hue and cry would be set up as soon as her abduction was known, and if caught the culprit wouldn't be granted the protection of law; he would be hanged from the nearest tree.

So now he didn't waste words in discussion with the man he knew as Thomas Cartwright, nor did he issue another warning to the struggling girl or hammer her with a heavy slap as she lay in front of him across his horse. That had been her punishment the first time he'd found it necessary to draw rein. Now, he grabbed her by the collar of her yellow shirt and with a sudden jerk, cast her on to the ground. She squealed, a mixture of surprise and pain, but Barclay ignored her.

'If you want her, you carry her,' he snarled at his companion. Because his mount was carrying double it was tiring more quickly than Cartwright's. He was handicapped if they were forced into a long run. 'You were crazy to bring her along. If you'd stuck to the plan we wouldn't have any fear of pursuit. It would have been days before news of our disappearance got back to the people of Mortimer. Not even the Texas Rangers would have been able to pick up our trail.'

'Take it easy,' replied Cartwright. 'No one is pursuing us. You don't think the stage driver and his side-kick will follow us, do you? Even if they were the heroic type, they have a schedule to keep and you know how stage people are devoted to their timetable.'

'She's slowing us down,' argued Barclay, 'and no woman is worth going to the gallows for.'

Cartwright's reply was in a thoughtful tone, rich in consideration of the other's words. 'What do you suggest?'

'Leave her here. Finding her unharmed might well blunt their urge to hunt for us. Let's keep riding and enjoy the money far away from this place.'

'But Sol, there isn't a posse on our trail. We have time to enjoy the girl and the money.'

Sol Barclay didn't agree. An instinct, an unexplainable caution nagged him, telling him it was dangerous to dawdle. Experience had taught him to ride fast and hard if he wanted to avoid the law.

'If you want her company then I say we split the money here and we'll go our separate ways.'

'If that's the way you want it,' Cartwright said, 'then that's what we'll do. I believe we agreed a sum of one thousand dollars.'

'That was before I took care of the Texas Rangers and hired those fellows to kill Jefferson.'

'They failed,' Cartwright reminded him.

'Only in killing Jefferson. Killing the sheriff created the same situation, one you could use to spur the town councillors into action.'

'Perhaps you're right.' Cartwright sounded affable. 'Let's make it two thousand dollars.'

'Let's make it half the contents of the bag,' snapped Barclay. 'You haven't any other partner because I got rid of him, too.'

Cartwright chuckled as he dismounted. 'You're quite right. Where would I be without you. You deserve a proper share of what's in the bag.'

Had Cartwright's easy acceptance of the demand not already triggered Sol's suspicion of the other's true intent, then the chuckle was the final proof. During their association of several weeks, Cartwright had been domineering, never giving an inch in argument or showing an iota of comrade-ship. He'd used Barclay like a tool and the possession of a bagful of money was unlikely to alter that. So, when Cartwright lifted the bag off the saddle horn and turned towards Barclay he found himself facing a man with a gun in his hand.

'Sol,' Cartwright protested, 'surely you don't think I intend to double-cross you?'

'Let's just say that I want to remove that tempta-tion.'

Cartwright held out the bag. 'You open it,' he said. 'There's only money inside. No guns.'

Tentatively, Barclay reached out to take the bag with his left hand, but until it was in his grasp his eyes never wavered from watching Cartwright. A low fork in an old tree provided a suitable place for him to balance the bag, enabling him to reach inside where the wads of paper money felt good in his hand. Now he smiled at the prospect of living well in a distant town. A movement caught his eye and his finger tightened on the trigger, but relaxed again almost immediately. His first reaction had been to suspect an attack from Cartwright but the movement had come from behind that big man. It was the girl, who had seen an opportunity to escape, darting swiftly to the shelter of some boulders where she hoped to evade her captors.

Sammy Sutton was unimportant to Barclay so he said nothing about her flight, but his eyes had alerted Cartwright who acknowledged her absence after a swift glance over his shoulder.

'She won't get far,' he said. 'But perhaps you're right, Sol, perhaps this is as far as she needs to go.'

'If you can find her,' said Barclay, his attention now more and more focused on the contents of the bag.'

'Where can she go? How far can she get without a horse?' Cartwright's voice was soft, assuring, made Barclay forget his suspicion that the man would be loath to part with any of the loot, particularly when he added, 'After we've sorted matters between ourselves then I'll settle with her.'

Sol's earlier suspicion, that when he dismounted it had been Cartwright's intention to kill him, had been accurate. However the weapon that Cartwright intended to use wasn't in the money

144

bag. Instead, it was a small derringer, which the big man carried in an inside pocket. Surreptitiously, when he'd turned away to look for Sammy Sutton, his right hand had slipped inside his jacket and retrieved the small gun. Barclay looked up as the big man stepped forward but barely recognized the threat to his life until the light report and brief flame of the discharged pistol coincided with the thump against his chest that caused him to totter backwards.

Instinctively, as he fell, Barclay pulled the trigger of the gun in his own hand, but the bullet went high into the night sky. He knew that he needed to get back on his feet, defend himself, shoot his gun at his attacker, but his body felt numb, his muscles were useless, his brain was unable to order the necessary commands. A face appeared above him. An enemy who had him at his mercy, whose foot was standing on the wrist that held his gun.

'You shouldn't have been greedy, Sol,' said Cartwright. 'I'm the one who decides each man's share and here is yours.' Cartwright fired the second bullet from the derringer into Barclay's forehead, killing him instantly.

From the refuge of a rock crevice, Samantha Sutton heard the gunshots. Although they were, at that moment, unexpected, she wasn't really surprised by them. She, like Sol Barclay, had been suspicious of Thomas Cartwright's affability with regard to sharing the money. She didn't believe he was the sort of man who cared about the fortunes of other people and was well aware of the fate he had planned for her. After the third shot, little more than a light plop puncturing the stillness of the night, there had been neither movement nor sound to indicate what was happening.

For several moments she waited, considering the possible outcomes of the showdown. She figured that if Cartwright had been killed by the man in black then the killer had most likely ridden away with the money, wouldn't be looking for her. But she hadn't heard any hoof beats, which would have confirmed his departure. If Cartwright had killed the other man then he would be hunting her, but she hadn't heard footfalls on the rocky ground or any indication of movement or search.

Perhaps, she thought, they'd shot each other and were lying dead or dying in the clearing. If so, she had only to mount one of the horses and ride back to the safety of the stage station. She waited in uninterrupted silence for another minute, then emerged from her hiding-place and began, carefully, to trace her route back to where the horses waited.

Reaching a point which gave her a clear view of the clearing, she paused. Bright moonlight illuminated the scene and she could see the placid horses with trailing reins waiting patiently for their next command. One of them turned its head in her direction as though a breeze had carried her scent, but it made no sound and soon lost interest. There were two other shapes on the ground, one on his back, arms outspread, over by the tree where the man in black had opened the money bag. The other was nearer the horses, on his side, curled in on himself as though trying to ease an intense pain in his stomach. Samantha waited and watched until she was sure that neither man was moving.

Even so, she approached with caution. The horses shuffled and one of them snorted a welcome when she reached them. Her first instinct was to climb into a saddle and ride with all haste back to the home of Dave Champion and his father but, even though she had no wish to stay any longer than was necessary, another thought brought about a change of mind. There was a carpetbag full of money to recover. She had last seen it in the fork of the tree, but clearly it was no longer balanced there. Reluctant to look at the bodies, she skirted around them as she crossed over to the tree to see if the bag had fallen to the ground. It wasn't behind the tree or anywhere in view.

Anxious to quit the place, Samantha resolved to leave the recovery of the money to whoever came to collect the bodies. If it was stolen money then somebody would be looking for it.

When she emerged from behind the tree Thomas Cartwright stood before her.

'I knew you would come back for a horse,' he

said, 'all I had to do was lie down and wait.'

Samantha looked at the body by the tree, saw the small hole in the forehead and knew that there was no help to be had from that quarter. Momentarily, fear gripped her. It was clear that Cartwright was a ruthless man, determined to have everything he wanted. The dark look in his eye confirmed that his want of her was now paramount.

When Barclay had thrown her from across his saddle she had hit the ground with the same shoulder that she'd hurt when getting a rifle to Charlie Jefferson during the shootout on Mortimer's main street. Now it nagged, as did the bruise on her jaw where Cartwright had punched her But, rather than weaken her, these things only strengthened her resolve, and although afraid, she was not terrified into inactivity. Whatever Cartwright did to her it wouldn't be done without a fight.

Dipping her right shoulder as though she meant to run in that direction where there were trees and bushes that might offer a hiding-place, she bent low and moved instead to her left. Her target was the gun she'd seen still clenched in the dead man's hand. If she could reach it she could yet escape from her attacker. She wasn't a stranger to guns, her father had taught her to handle them from a young age.

But despite his size, Cartwright could also move quickly. Tricked at first by the girl's feint, he recovered quickly, making a grab for, her but she ducked under his lunge. Turning to give chase, he immediately understood the girl's intention: the gun barrel was bright in the moonlight. He shouted as she dived to the ground and rolled towards the weapon. Swiftly he covered the ground between them, got his hands on her shoulders and tried to pull her away. He felt a pain in his shin as she kicked backwards to defend herself.

Samantha reached for the gun, got her hand around the barrel and tried to pull it towards her, but it was held in a dead man's grip and didn't come free easily. She felt Cartwright's hands on her arms, tried to resist his effort to drag her away but he was very strong and although she struggled valiantly her resistance was doomed to failure. But she clung to the pistol and when she was lifted off Sol Barclay's body the gun was in her hand.

Cartwright shook her violently until she dropped the gun, then he cast her aside so that she hit the ground with stunning force. He picked up the gun and cursed.

'I should just finish you now,' he said, and pulled back the hammer to emphasize his words.

In headlong pursuit, the little pinto had proved to be as swift as Charlie Jefferson had hoped. She had run flat out for almost thirty minutes without faltering but Charlie knew he would have to slow down soon to give the beast a rest. They had followed the natural contours of the land, climbing where necessary as they followed the tracks that he hoped were made by his prey.

He had descended into a dry depression when the sounds of three gunshots reached him from beyond the next ridge. He wasn't sure that the first sound had been a gunshot, being light, as though from a toy gun, but the second had been the full-throated roar of a forty-five, unmistakable even though it was distorted by the echo in the emptiness of the hills. He touched his spurs once more to the pinto's flanks and asked it to climb again.

At first when he reached the summit there was nothing to see. Reluctant to rush headlong into a situation that could bring harm to Samantha Sutton, Charlie dismounted and began to descend, moving from rock cover to rock cover but all the time scanning the territory ahead. He saw the horses first, then the body by the tree. It wasn't until he moved again and was halfway down the slope that he saw the second shape on the ground; he figured it must have been obscured from view earlier by the horses. He knew that both bodies were too big to be Samantha and he wondered what had happened to her.

The hillside rock formations had been an advantage during his descent from the ridge, hiding him from anyone in the depression, but they had also worked against him, had prevented him from seeing a permanent view of what lay below. So it wasn't until he reached level ground that he glimpsed Samantha's bright-yellow shirt. She was twenty yards away, near a tree where she was being confronted by the man he knew as Farraday.

Suddenly she moved, evading Farraday's lunge before diving to the ground. Charlie had his gun in his hand and would have fired, but by this time Farraday was holding Samantha, was shaking her then throwing her to the ground. At last he stood over her, holding a gun which he cocked.

'Farraday,' yelled Charlie Jefferson.

Farraday looked up, surprised to hear his name in this remote place but recognizing instantly the challenge and threat in the utterance of that one word. He turned the readied weapon in the direction of the voice. It was his last conscious movement.

Charlie Jefferson fired twice, both bullets finding their target. Farraday was flung backwards to come to rest against the old forked tree. In a moment Charlie was at Samantha's side, lifting her to her feet and examining her for signs of injury.

Later, as he loaded the horses with the bodies of their dead masters, he found the bag of money tied to the saddle on one of the animals. With Samantha mounted on her pinto, Charlie, walking, led the way back to the relay station. On the way they met the posse that had been organized by Horry Blackmore and the mayor. Henry Sutton was riding with them.

'You've got a brave daughter,' Charlie told

Sutton, but it was clear that that meant little to him compared to the fact that she was safe and going home.

CHAPTER THIRTEEN

Charlie Jefferson didn't see Samantha Sutton again until he was quitting the territory two days later. In that time he had again been courted by the town committee to accept their vacant position for a sheriff but it didn't need a moment's thought for him to refuse. It crossed his mind that his rapid appointment would merely be a means of distracting the townspeople from their criticism of the mayor and his friends, who had almost led the town into a dire situation. At another public meeting they admitted that they had been duped, that the railway men with whom they'd been in contact had turned out to be bogus officials introduced by Farraday and that, although their desire for the development of Mortimer still burned strongly, it would be a long time before they launched the town into another enterprise.

However, what Charlie had done for Mortimer didn't go unrewarded. All the money was returned to everyone who had contributed to the scheme and in addition to a $500 reward from the town funds, he received other, personal gifts. Chief among them was a deep-chested, grey gelding from Curt Templeton which had been his pride and was renowned throughout the territory for its speed and stamina. To complement his brother's gift, Joel Templeton had harnessed the horse with a fine Mexican style saddle and accoutrements all decorated with silver conchas. Oliver Calloway, who probably owed most to Charlie because he'd invested the bank's money without approval, presented him with the best rifle he could buy from the town's gun shop.

For two days Charlie was toasted wherever he went in Mortimer. No one asked for payment for his hotel room, restaurant fare, barroom drinks or barber services, There were many who thought Charlie crazy for not taking advantage of his celebrity status for longer, but Charlie told everyone that he was going home and that nothing could change his mind.

To the surprise of most people, not least Doctor Spenser, Tom Chisum survived the knife wound. When Charlie visited the Ranger he was told that he would receive a $1,000 reward for the capture of Courtney Farraday. Charlie said that the money should go to Samantha Sutton, who had done just as much to bring Farraday to justice.

*

It seemed that word of his approach had already been brought to the ranch house by one of the Sutton hands, because when he rode into the yard on Smoke, the grey, leading the animal borrowed from their stock, Samantha was on the porch watching for him.

'I'm returning your horse,' he said.

She wore a dress, a plain greyish-blue affair that she probably wore when she was busy in the kitchen or tidying the house, not something intended as a feminine weapon. Her chin was high and she smiled although, it seemed, with difficulty, yet her eyes were clear and her voice was strong and level.

'Is that your only reason for being here?'

'No. I came to tell you I was leaving. Came to say goodbye.'

Her lips tightened before she spoke again. 'And to share a meal, I daresay. That invitation was extended the last time you were here.'

Charlie remembered her words well, sit at table with us, and he remembered too, wondering how her father would react to such a suggestion. At that moment the door behind Samantha opened and Henry Sutton strode out on to the veranda.

'Jefferson,' the rancher said in greeting and in that one word Charlie sensed a different attitude, as though for the first time, Henry Sutton didn't regard him as a worthless drifter.

'Mr Jefferson is here to eat with us,' his daughter told him.

155

'Well, step down and come inside,' said Sutton, and Charlie had no option but to obey. 'Is that Curt Templeton's grey?' enquired the rancher.

'It was. He gave him to me, and the harness is from his brother.'

'Well, you earned them, boy,' Sutton said. 'The town would be bankrupt if you hadn't been around.'

'I didn't do anything,' Charlie told him modestly. 'My involvement was an accident.'

Henry Sutton dismissed those words with a wave of his hand. 'I'm not forgetting what you did for my daughter, either. I owe you a lot.'

'Anything I did merely goes part way to cancel out what she did for me. I wouldn't have been around to help her if she hadn't saved my life in Mortimer.'

The meal was a simple affair. There was chicken which that morning might have been scuttling about the yard, and potatoes and vegetables which, no doubt, had been grown in their own garden plot. Henry Sutton asked about Charlie's plans and was clearly taken aback by the news that he was heading for Wyoming.

'I've been heading that way since the end of the war,' Charlie confided. 'Haven't seen my folks for eight years.'

A look passed between father and daughter that reeked of disappointment.

'Will you come back this way?' Sutton asked. 'I

was aiming to make you an offer to come here, learn the cattle business beyond roping and branding.'

Charlie grinned. His father had been raising cattle since Charlie was a lad. He already knew the cattle business but he knew he would never convince a Texan about that.

'You never know what else it might lead to,' added Henry Sutton, and again his eyes flicked towards his daughter.

'I appreciate the offer,' Charlie told him, 'but I don't believe I can change my plans.' An uncomfortable silence hung around the threesome until Charlie rose and thanked them for the meal. 'I mean to call on the Champions, then get a few miles north before it becomes too dark to travel.'

'You'll want to collect your horse,' said Samantha 'He's well rested.'

The big red was in a corral at the side of the house and he trotted over when Charlie climbed on to the gate. As they stroked his head, Charlie told Samantha that when he got to Wyoming he expected to marry Ruth Prescott. She had sworn to wait for him when he went to war and he had no reason to believe she hadn't.

'Will you keep Red?' he asked her. 'Perhaps if you ride him out now and then you'll remember me.'

'What makes you think I won't remember you?' she asked; then, in a different tone, added 'What makes you think I want to remember you?'

'I guess I just hoped you would because you're the bravest girl I've ever known, and I know I'll remember you.'

She turned away, buried her face against Red's neck and stayed there while Charlie walked away.

Dave Champion was in the same position he'd been in when Charlie first saw him: perched on a rail blowing notes out of his tin whistle. When he saw Charlie he jumped down and ran to greet him and to voice his admiration for the new horse and saddle.

'I can see that you are fully recovered,' Charlie said 'How is your father?'

'Doctor says it'll be several weeks before he can do any heavy work but he'll be OK. Harry Goater from the office in Mortimer sent someone out to help with the work here.'

John Champion was very pale but he was pleased to see Charlie Jefferson even though it was a farewell visit.

'Despite the mayhem you brought with you I think a lot of people will be sorry to see you go. Harry Goater told me that you were the popular choice to replace Abe Agnew as sheriff.'

'I'm not sure I'd make a good sheriff. I had personal reasons for hunting down those men. One had stolen my horse and Farraday had kidnapped Samantha Sutton. I wasn't interested in whether or not he escaped with the town's money.'

Dave Champion told his father about Charlie's new horse and equipment. 'You should see the saddle,' he enthused, 'it's covered in silver discs.'

'Well, it'll be worth more than that old thing you persuaded us to recover when you were first here. It was so old and worn I don't know how anyone could stay astride their mount.'

Charlie recalled John and his son riding out towards Cleary's Canyon, hoping to salvage a saddle and rifle from Harker's dead horse. A sudden thought gave him hope.

'Was the saddle still on the dead beast?'

'No, it had been removed and cast aside.'

'What did you do with it?'

'We brought it back here. We'd gone all the way to Cleary's Canyon so we weren't keen to return empty handed.'

'Have you still got it?'

'It's with the rest of the tack in the wagon shed.'

Dave went along with Charlie to seek out the old saddle. Charlie recognized it immediately. He picked it up and, like John Champion had said, it was in barely usable condition, but it was his and he could feel the thick paper bonds behind the cloth under-lining. Harker, he realized, had returned to his dead horse to change saddles before riding on to Mortimer.

'Let's swap,' Charlie told a delighted Dave Champion. 'You can have that rig, which is too fancy for me, and I'll take back my old saddle.'

159

Dave Champion was happily playing what he believed was *Buffalo Gals* as Charlie Jefferson began his journey north, back to his Wyoming home in the valley of the Tatanka.